STRESS FAMILY ROBINSON 2

Adrian Plass

STRESS FAMILY ROBINSON 2
The Birthday Party

Marshall Pickering
An Imprint of HarperCollinsPublishers

Marshall Pickering is an imprint of
HarperCollins*Religious*
Part of HarperCollins*Publishers*
77–85 Fulham Palace Road, London W6 8JB
www.christian-publishing.com

First published in Great Britain in 1999 by HarperCollins*Publishers*
This edition published in 2000 by Marshall Pickering

1 3 5 7 9 10 8 6 4 2

A catalogue record for this book
is available from the British Library.

ISBN 0 551 03108 5

Printed and bound in Great Britain by
Caledonian International Book Manufacturing Ltd, Glasgow

Contents

Saturday

1

'Kathy Robinson,' I muttered to myself, 'you seem to have arrived in hell a little before your time.'

It was just after seven o'clock, the beginning of one of those long, bad days when everything smells of fish. Mind you, it followed a Friday night that had smelled even worse of failure. I woke at least four times, always with the same negative thought rolling uselessly round and round in my brain like the proverbial marble in a cake-tin. The last one had been at about three thirty in the morning, when such an oppressive weight of despair pressed on me in the darkness of the bedroom that in the end I had to slip out of bed and escape, leaving Mike, my husband, fast asleep.

Resonant nasal sounds issued reassuringly from behind the closed door of our older son Jack's room as I tiptoed along the landing trying not to wake the rest of the household, and it would have been a waste of energy worrying about his brother Mark, who slept in the big room right up on the second floor. Mark, recently turned eighteen, had consistently demonstrated a capacity bordering on the supernatural for remaining asleep in the face of any and every disturbance.

At the angle of the stairs I paused by the open

doorway of my daughter's room. No problem there either. Felicity was sleeping at a friend's house for the night. She was ten, as wide open as that door of hers, and still quite convinced that she lived in the best of all possible worlds. In the light filtering through the curtains from a streetlamp outside, I could see her favourite old teddy sitting patiently on the pillow waiting for his mistress to return. Felicity had phoned the evening before to say what a good time she was having. She would be fast asleep now. I sighed, glad for her, but sorry for myself.

Downstairs in the strange, alien world of the early hours I made a cup of tea and tuned in to one of those Sky channels that American evangelists buy slots on at that time of the morning, hoping to comfort myself with the knowledge that there were one or two people in the world who might be even loonier than me. I eventually got back to sleep just before five.

Continually waking at night is bad for me, but not half as bad as it's likely to be for those who are favoured with my presence the next day. I may have slightly miscounted, but, as far as my blessedly selective memory can recall, I went on to offend or upset at least five people before teatime on Saturday. Those who love me have been kind and helpful enough to explain that I have an abrasive quality at the best of times, but this must have been a record, even for me.

The person who headed this queue of applicants for verbal abuse was brave or foolish enough to present herself on the telephone shortly after the alarm went at seven o'clock, a time when I am only embryonically human at best. I desire no companion then, other than strong, sweet coffee, made by me, just the way I like it. It was my turn to get up first to make sure that Mark was stirring in his lair, and although Mike would have understood if I'd prodded him awake and begged for a swop, I simply had not been able to face that infernal negative revolution again, so I got up. Slumped at the kitchen table after giving my son a call and receiving the statutory moan of irrational resentment and understandable agony in reply, I had just spooned the second sugar into my mug, and was on the point of stirring it before taking my first sip of the morning, when the telephone rang.

That was the moment when I thought I might have entered eternal torment without realizing it.

Those of you who have read about our exploits of a few years ago* will be aware that we Robinsons have raised the art of confusion and absurdity to new, rarefied heights. What followed on this occasion was quite up to our normal standard. I waited for half a minute or so, then, uttering an oath of pagan pungency, I put my mug down and huffed into the hall to answer the infuriatingly insistent ringing. As I picked up the receiver and barked 'Hello!' into it, Mike did exactly the same (well, he did more of a polite little 'woof' than a bark) on the extension phone that lives in a small alcove next to

---

* See *Stress Family Robinson*, HarperCollins, 1995.

my side of our double bed. Hearing Mike answer I grunted with relief, dropped the phone back on its thingy, and returned to my coffee, which was still just about hot enough to get the revival process going again.

This would have been fine if Mike hadn't done exactly the same thing upstairs. For a minute and a half we both enjoyed the satisfaction of believing that our early-morning caller was being dealt with by the other person, then the silence was shattered once more by the ringing of the telephone. I could hardly believe it! Who was calling now? Once again I waited for it to stop. Once again it didn't. Once again there was a spooky synchronicity about the way in which Mike and I picked up our receivers and replied at exactly the same time. Once again we both replaced the phone and returned to our respective dozing and coffee-drinking.

Two minutes later, when the phone went for a third time, I felt cross to the point of snarling. Why had everybody in the entire world elected, one by one, to call at some unearthly hour of the morning, inflicting telephonic Chinese water torture on two innocent people? Just how stupid was it possible for the entire world to be? I decided that it would be far better to let Mike answer the call this time as I would find it very difficult to avoid being openly aggressive.

Isn't it interesting how immediately identifiable a certain amalgam of sounds can be? 'Getting out of bed in an infuriated state to come and give someone a piece of your mind' is one good example. First, there's a sort of 'Hurrumph!' of annoyance followed by a flapping and a slapping of bedclothes, then the thumping sound of a pair of feet landing with unnecessary force on the bedroom floor before they stomp irritably across the room and along the landing towards the top of the stairs. There might be a slammed door thrown in as well, according to choice.

'It is your turn to get up, isn't it, Kath?'

Mike almost always stops short of really expressing his anger. He screeches to a halt on the edge of rage, like someone nearly driving a Volvo estate over Beachy Head. I think it frightens him. That's why, on this bad-fish morning, the flapping and stomping actually culminated in a question of such reedy restraint from the top of the stairs. If it had been me I would have come flying downstairs like a loosely tied bag of laundry and burst indiscriminately over everyone in sight. Mike's question was a coded statement, an all too familiar attempt on his part to insert a skeleton of order into the flabby, chaotic flesh of what was actually happening. He went on to expand his point with that very particular brand of schoolmasterish heavy patience of his that maddens me more than almost anything else he does. It wouldn't have been so bad if he had come downstairs and spoken to me on the same physical level. Being addressed sternly from the top of the stairs by a junior headmaster makes you feel like the school assembly hearing that a few of us are letting the rest of us down, or perhaps like a failed pilgrim being told off by God in a morality play.

'Kathy, we have an arrangement, have we not, that we'll take it in turns to be the first to get up in the morning, and this morning it was your turn, so I stayed in bed. In the half hour or so between you getting up and me getting up, you know that if anything happens it's your concern. I happily take that responsibility when it's my turn, so why can't you? My only responsibility this morning is to make the bed when I *do* get up. Each time the phone has gone this morning, I have optimistically hung on to the tail-end of my dream and gritted my teeth waiting for you to answer it. You know full well that the phone is just beyond leaning reach from my side, so to get to it I have to support myself with one hand on the floor, and pick up the phone with the other. I don't *like* doing that. Each time it's rung, you've delayed answering just long enough for me to give up waiting and feel like screaming and have to throw my body across to your side of the bed and answer it myself. Then you put the phone down as soon as you hear me speak, presumably not real-izing that I have put mine down as well. Dreams don't survive all that, Kathy. Whoever has been trying to call is now ringing for the *third* time.' His voice rose to a strangled pitch. 'Please, *please* will you answer it, so I can go back to bed for the tiny little bit of time that's left? I hope you don't think I'm being too unreasonable.'

Stomp, stomp, stomp, slam, boing, flap!

The process by which my mind roots around to find logical justification for my misdeeds is a shamefully industrious one. I can't believe that I

am capable of putting so much mental effort into
being right at times when I know perfectly well I'm
wrong. As I picked up the still-ringing phone from
the hall table and put it to my ear, I was busy con-
structing arguments with which to slay Mike over
the marmalade a little later.

'Yes?'

My Basil Fawlty-like tone of voice can hardly
have sounded very welcoming, but some people
are pretty well immune to tones of voice.

'Oh, Kathy, is that you? Joscelyn here – I had a
bit of trouble getting through just now. Listen, I
know it's early, dear, but I just had to ring you to
pass on the good news. I was sure you'd want
to hear.'

I knew the deep, female voice well. Joscelyn
Wayne was a member of our church, one of those
people who make the very joints of your body ache
because it's virtually impossible to react honestly to
them. At least, that was the problem I had with her.

She was a large, handsome woman with, in the
best cartoon tradition, a small submissive husband
called John. When they were first introduced to
Mike and me as a couple I suffered one of those
embarrassingly explicit nasal extrusions on hearing
that I was in the presence of a cottage-sized John
Wayne.

I remember the same thing happening once
when I was introduced to an elderly man who
happened to have his back to me at the time. When
he turned round the first thing I noticed was his
nose. I couldn't help it. No one could have helped

it. He was wearing a large, shiny, blatantly obvious plastic nose. Trapped helplessly between the only two feasible options, that it was this person's idea of a practical joke or that he was undergoing some kind of nasal treatment that demanded a temporary replacement, I fell to pieces and produced a similar snorting explosion – through my nose, of course. Our chat was a trifle strained after that, I seem to recall.

Poor John Wayne was obviously used to this kind of childish reaction, because he just smiled with his eyes, offered me a tissue that he fished out from somewhere, and said mildly, 'Don't worry, it is funny. Don't quite match up, do I? The hell I do!'

I felt terrible after that, but as time went by I discovered that little John really was very nice, and quite drily funny when his wife wasn't filling the horizon. They really were an extraordinary contrast in size. He was neatly dressed and nicely made, as far as one could see, whereas she was one of those women who wear their hair long a bit too late in life, and you can't quite tell where their flowing clothes end and their flowing bodies begin. I suppose you shouldn't conjecture about other people's sex lives, but – no, well, I've already said it, haven't I – you shouldn't, should you?

Joscelyn was a seeker after spiritual adventure, one who, as my son Jack once graphically put it, runs frantically round pushing an open wheely-bin, trying to work out exactly where the blessing is going to fall. A strange mixture of self-assurance and neediness, Joscelyn wrote exhortational articles for Christian magazines, and was in demand as a speaker at ladies' meetings in various parts of the country. I drove her to one of these once and was amazed at the confidence with which she offered hands-on ministry to a large group of posh-ish women. Many of them moved from chintzy, tea-sipping ordinariness to tearful, crumpled collapse and back again, and they did it in a bewilderingly seamless manner. One of the problems I had with our relationship from that day onward was the assumption in Joscelyn that I had been deeply awed and moved by what I had seen at that meeting. In fact, my overwhelming response had been troubled puzzlement.

In her writing, and in the one example of her public speaking that I had witnessed, Joscelyn projected a bright-eyed definiteness about the presence and power and closeness of God that must have been inspiring to many of her readers and listeners. The trouble was, I didn't really believe that what came out of her had ever been *in* her, if you see what I mean. It seemed to me that the person she was actually trying to convince about the reality of God was herself. Perhaps that was all right. I didn't know. What I did know was that, in her case, you didn't have to be deeply insightful to detect the fundamental panic that fuelled this constant outpouring of spiritual optimism and confidence.

Every few weeks Joscelyn would announce with great excitement that somewhere she had been or something she had done had enabled God to do a completely new thing in her, and that, as a result, her entire life was changed for the better. I should have reacted more honestly in the early days, when she first said these sorts of things to me and all I felt was a gnawing scepticism. Now, hampered by my long history of chickening out, all I could do each time was squeeze little bleating noises of approval out of my mouth, indulging the child inside Joscelyn who needed such huge dollops of self-deception in order to survive. And that, as my dear husband will tell you – and he certainly would tell you if you were to ask him – is the trouble with people like me. We only seem to have two modes of response in situations like that, rudeness or collusion.

There is, however, nothing like chronic fatigue and disgust with oneself for provoking rudeness to others. I sensed that I was about to change modes in my interaction with Joscelyn.

'What news would that be then, Joscelyn?'

'Oh, Kathy, I have had *the* most amazing time at Falston Manor over the weekend. God really did – look, you don't mind me ringing you this early, do you? John said I ought to leave it an hour or so, but I said you'd be dying to hear how it went.'

'John was right, Joscelyn.'

'Oh, good,' said the voice on the other end of the line, 'I told him you wouldn't mind.'

I was fairly used to Joscelyn not appearing to actually hear what I said, but on this fishy morning it infuriated me beyond measure. What on earth was the matter with the woman that she didn't even register the words I spoke? I had often had the feeling that I was superfluous to our conversations. I might as well have been a stuffed dummy equipped with a tape-loop and loud-speakers for all the genuine interest that she showed in my responses. Joscelyn knew exactly what she expected my reaction to be, and never bothered to stop and check whether she was up the creek or not. Well – okay! Right! This was where things were going to start changing.

'I don't think you can have heard what I said, Joscelyn. I said that –'

'They had the most marvellous speaker for the weekend, someone called Brian Wills from some-where in the Leicester area, although he goes all over the place, apparently. Have you come across him? He's written two books. I bought them while I was there and I *must* lend you the first one and a tape of the Saturday evening session from this weekend. He writes just like he speaks, which is quite unusual, isn't it?'

I decided to try again.

'Joscelyn, this is not the –'

Like a panzer division with its periscopes misted up, she rolled blindly on.

'Kathy, this man has a ministry to leaders that is truly anointed – *truly* anointed. I have never, *ever* felt the sheer power of God as I felt it on that Saturday night in the session before the entertain-ment. The very air crackled with – with, well, with the sheer power of God. At the end Brian asked all those who wanted prayer to come up to the front and form a line, and then he prayed and prophe-sied over each of us, one by one. People were going down and getting filled with the Spirit and being healed, and Kathy, he said things to me that went right down deep inside and were literally life-changing. I tell you what, God has totally trans-formed me over this weekend in the most *amazing* way, and—'

'Joscelyn, Joscelyn, what *are* you talking about?'

This time I got through, probably because I had projected the words down the telephone line with as much vim as I could muster, and then some. Joscelyn, arrested at last, sounded puzzled by my question.

'Sorry – what do you mean? What are you – why are you asking me what I'm talking about? I'm telling you what happened at the weekend.'

'I mean, Joscelyn, that just about every month or so since I first met you, you've rung me up or come round to tell me about your life being *totally* changed by someone or something in the most *amazing* way. But you always appear to me to be exactly the same as you were before it happened. I mean, let's face it, if you really had been radically altered and transformed by God as many times as you reckon you have been, then there can't be much of the original you left, can there? You must be Elmat Zog from the planet Vorgan by now.'

'But I—'

'What you probably really mean,' I continued mercilessly, 'what you almost certainly are actually saying is that you've simply moved another small but important step towards understanding that you're a sinner like the rest of us and that God forgives you.'

Suddenly the things I'd thought but never said during those other conversations welled up inside me and poured out. I had said it all in my head so many times. It was like reading a finely-honed script.

'Why you have to dress it up in all this "totally transformed" rubbish is beyond me. Do you not realize that what you're actually talking about all the time is *you*? That's what Christians do, Joscelyn. We all do it. *I* do it. I'm just the same. I go on and on and on about myself and *my* standing with God, and how *I'm* doing, and how far *I've* got, and all the time God is trying to get a word in edgeways so that he can say, "Look, it's not about you – it's about me and what I've done for you. Stop navel-gazing and look in my direction because I've already saved your blinking navel, just as I've saved every other part of you. That's the good news. The bad news is that you're never going to be this wonderful person you seem to think you have to be before I notice that you exist." What you need, Joscelyn, if you don't mind me saying so, is to learn how to relax.'

With this final, grotesquely hypocritical piece of advice from me, the least relaxed person in the universe, I terminated my sermon, and a profound silence fell at both ends of the line. It was broken at my end by the sound of the doorbell ringing. I was more than relieved to have such a genuine exit presented to me.

'Look, Joscelyn, I'm going to have to go, there's someone at the door. You're not upset by what I said, are you?'

'No, no ...'

'Well, look, I'll give you a call later, all right?'

'All right ...'

A tiny voice. I had never heard Joscelyn sounding so deflated and defeated. I replaced the receiver on its hook with agonized deliberateness. What had I done? Who did I think I was? What would Mike say when he heard that I'd tried to snuff out Joscelyn's spiritual confidence as though it was a cheap candle? I sighed as I suddenly remembered that my friend, Dip Reynolds, was coming round for coffee later that morning because she had something important to tell me. Another potential victim? Perhaps I'd be more human by then. Dip always had a good effect on me.

When I opened the door our new milk-delivery girl was standing with a crate on the step by her feet, holding a little sheaf of bits of thin paper in her hand. She was a young, skinny, almost very pretty girl with large trusting eyes, an oval face and a coil of black hair dangling on to each cheek. There was a very earnest expression on her face. Since taking over the franchise for our round a few weeks ago, she had developed a new method of giving out bills and collecting money which was supposed to make the paying-for-milk side of our lives much easier for her and for all of us, her customers. I was absolutely open to the proposition that it might have made life much easier if we had ever managed to understand it, but neither Mike nor I had been able to grasp the new system at all, despite having invited the girl in one Saturday morning to sit down in the kitchen and explain it to us.

Mind you, this was as much to do with us as her – more, probably. Mike has quite a clear head for most things, but, thank God, we share a chronic inability to understand what people are talking about when they address us at any speed above a crawl on subjects that involve money.

This had certainly been the case several years ago, when we were in the middle of buying the tall, thin, three-storey Victorian house within which we now scuttled up and down from trough to sleeping areas and back again like a family of neurotic hamsters.

The man who dealt with our mortgage might as well have spoken the language of a lost South American tribe as far as the gaping, dull-brained Robinsons were concerned. Every few minutes, when our broker stopped to take a breath, Mike, optimistically armed with a pad of paper and a biro and trying to sound like a grown-up, would say rather plaintively, 'So, what's likely to be the total we pay each month?' Then the man would reluctantly name a figure, which Mike would write down, and after an immaculately timed pause the man would casually add that, of course, this didn't include two or three other expensive but vitally essential items that he would mention later, and Mike would cross out the amount he had just written down on his pad and run his hand wildly through his hair, and look as if he was going to ask another question, but by then the man would have started talking again, and it would be another few minutes before it became possible to go through the whole routine once more. We ended up feeling like lobotomized chimpanzees in a ballet class.

There was an up-side to our encounters with this obscurantism, by the way. Smart as this young man presumably was, he had, in the course of his professional encounters with customers, unconsciously acquired the habit of beginning every other sentence with the phrase, 'Quite honestly'. As the time for our third meeting with him approached, we agreed, like a couple of naughty children, that, as we had not the faintest idea what he was talking about anyway, we might as well while away the hour or so spent in his company by counting the number of times he used this suspicious verbal ploy. (Mike can do this sort of mildly wicked thing when he tries, and I really love it when he does.) It must have been very gratifying for our broker that day to observe the way in which we hung on to his every word without once interrupting. I think the score had reached twenty-four by the time the meeting was about to draw to a close, and it was then that I decided to try an experiment.

'I hope you don't mind me asking,' I said innocently, 'it's pure curiosity on my part, but I was wondering if you actually come from around here?'

He cast a worried look in my direction, disconcerted, of course, by the near impossibility of coming up with a reply to my question that would

either cost us money or be impossible to understand. He did manage to twist his features into
more of a now-we're-talking-on-a-personal-level,
relaxed sort of expression, but there was nothing
he could do about the words that came out of his
mouth. His mouth knew no other formula.

'Quite honestly,' he said, as though confessing to
some sick and miserable vice, 'I live in Brighton.'

Inexplicable collapse of Robinsons. What, he
must have wondered, is so very amusing about
living in Brighton? Quite honestly, nothing ...

In the case of our new milkgirl and her system,
it was just the same. The more she talked, the less
we seemed to grasp what she was getting at, until,
in the end, lying was the only remaining option. So
we did. We sat back and flapped the air with our
hands, saying things like, 'Aaah, with you – right!
Now I see what you're saying. Yes, that is a *much*
better way of doing it! Gosh, that will make a difference!' and she went away pleased. Mike and I had
laughed a great deal about this at the time, but I
wasn't in the mood for humour or humouring
right now. This girl was number two in the victim
queue, or number three if you counted Mike as
number one.

I snapped, 'You want me to pay for the milk?'

'Not all of it,' she said, brushing one of the
dangling coils away from eyes that gleamed with
the joy of seeing her master-plan in action. 'If you
remember, Mrs Robinson, I said the best thing
would be if people where I collect on Saturdays go
from Tuesday to Tuesday in retrospect, so as you

were away until last Monday you only owe me for one day, unless you want to add it on to what you'll owe up to next Wednesday, in which case I won't take anything until the end of next week.'

I stared at her. Incredible! The remarkable thing about this modern deliverer of milk was that she obviously understood what she was saying. There was a logical pattern hidden away in there somewhere, forever inaccessible to a brain such as mine, but perfectly meaningful to her. I was quite awed in a way. The poor girl might have suffered only a morose dismissal if it hadn't been for Mark, who selected that very moment to bring his newly showered, dripping form stumbling comatosely down the stairs behind me, wrapped insubstantially in a stupidly small towel and clutching one of those horrible, floppy, unfunny joke-books that get progressively soggier in the bathroom until they finally congeal and die. Pausing unselfconsciously in the hall, in full view of those in the world outside our open front door, he read aloud from his cornucopia of rubbish.

'Did you hear about the constipated footballer who squeezed one through in stoppage time?'

Throwing his head back, Mark guffawed with such energy over this terrible so-called joke that he lost his one-handed grip on the towel and it dropped around his feet. This is pure conjecture, but my guess would be that for one eternal moment our milk-deliverer forgot even her new system as she stared open-mouthed at my naked son. Then, the towel was scooped up and the great comedian beat a hasty retreat to the safety of the kitchen. An all too familiar, Mark-related tide of hot fury rose in me as I turned once more to the embarrassed girl on the step.

'I'm afraid you've completely confused me about the money. Why don't you just come back next Saturday and tell us what we owe you and we'll pay it. I think we can all understand that. All right?'

And I shut the door on her. I hate myself sometimes.

At this moment, however, reflection was not the order of the day. Just now, I hated Mark much more than I hated myself, and I was determined that he was shortly going to hear about it in graphic detail. With my hand still resting on the closed door I screwed my eyes tight shut and took three or four deep breaths through my nose in an effort to dull the near berserk edge of my fury. One of my secret fears was that wild anger would one day cause me to totally wreck a room or a relationship or perhaps even a person, in the attempt to clearly communicate *just how cross I was!*

A voice from the kitchen called out in cheerful unawareness of Hurricane Kathy's imminent approach.

'Mum, could you bring us a bottle of that milk through for my cereal? Cheers!'

Could I bring ...? Right!

When I arrived in the kitchen Mark's inadequately betowelled figure was seated at the end of the table nearest the hall, in front of a large glass mixing bowl containing a miniature mountain range of five Shredded Wheat, surmounted by an additional Everest-like peak of sugar. He was tapping the table rhythmically and happily with a huge serving-spoon as he waited for me to arrive with supplies of the missing ingredient. For some reason the sight of the wrong kind of bowl with too much in it and that ludicrously large spoon had the effect of racking my annoyance up yet another notch. I leaned against the sink and folded my arms.

'Why are you using a mixing bowl and that spoon when we've got plenty of things the right size?'

'They're all in the dishwasher. Where's the milk?'

'So why didn't you take them out of the dish-washer?'

Silent pause.

'Come on! Why didn't you take everything out of the dishwasher and put it all away like I do just about every morning of my life? Why do you take that stupid great serving thing out of the drawer instead of getting one everybody else would use? No, don't wear yourself out answering. I'll tell you why – it's because you can't be bothered, that's why. It's too much like hard work, isn't it? And besides that, it might benefit other people, and the last thing we'd want to do is anything that might be useful to anybody else, isn't it? Silly of me to even think of it.'

Mark had stopped tapping with his spoon and was staring fixedly at the far end of the table.

Eventually, taking a deep breath and expelling it loudly through pursed lips, he rose to his feet, still hanging on to his towel, and turned towards the hall.

'I'll get the milk myself,' he mumbled.

'You will not get the milk yourself. Don't you think the world has seen enough of you already this morning? No, you're going to sit back down on that chair and listen to me!'

Mark debated inwardly for a moment then, slumping heavily back into his seat, he leaned his elbows on the table and rested his chin in his cupped hands.

'What's going on?'

Mike, presumably drawn by the rumblings of imminent conflict, appeared in the kitchen wearing my dressing-gown and his very own aggrieved-but-ready-to-listen expression.

I struggled to find appropriate words. I was so tired! For an annoying second or two I found that I had completely forgotten everything that had gone on just before coming into the kitchen. That's often a problem when you get as het up as I do. You lose track of your original, excellent reasons for being so angry, then all that gets talked about is the last thing you said and it sounds pathetic. That was exactly what happened now. Mark leaned back in his chair and spoke to his father in the sort of wearily ironic tone that a guard in an institution might use with a colleague to describe the boringly predictable irrationality of one of their long-term resident lunatics.

'Mum is really, really, really cross with me for using the wrong size of spoon with my cereal, so she won't let me get any milk for some reason.'

The common expression about people or events making your blood boil is horribly accurate. When, as Mark had just done, someone manages to scrabble all the loose ends of everything that's happened into a knot, and you know that, because you're so full of outrage, trying to explain will only pull it tighter, it does feel as if steam might well come shooting out of the top of your head. And I don't care if string and steam don't fit together, because that's how it feels.

'I have never heard anything quite so absurdly ridiculous in my life! You know perfectly well that I got cross with you because you told a stupid, vulgar joke in front of a strange girl standing on the step with no clothes on.'

'What! When was this?'

Mike's face was a picture of shock and bewilderment.

'Just now, at the bottom of the stairs.'

'Who was the strange girl?'

'The milkgirl – person, whatever you're supposed to call them nowadays. The girl with the impenetrable system who delivers our milk.'

'But she's not strange. We know her.'

'Oh, you know perfectly *well* what I mean! She's not – you know – one of the family.'

'But why was she standing on the step naked?'

'*What?*'

'Why was the girl naked?'

'She wasn't.'

'But you just said she was.'

'I did not!' I almost screamed, 'I said that Mark was naked. Mark! Your son! Watch my lips – MARK WAS NAKED IN THE HALL!'

'No I wasn't,' protested Mark indignantly, 'well, only when I hadn't got anything on.'

'Oh, sorry! I stupidly assumed that we might all agree on that as a reasonably accurate definition of nakedness.'

'No, I mean it was only for about half a second because my towel slipped off, and I didn't know she was there anyway, and in any case, it was an accident. And I wasn't telling *her* that joke, I was reading it to myself.'

'Ah, yes, but it's always an accident with you, isn't it, Mark? You never actually *mean* to do anything, do you?'

Why do I always feel as if I'm being bullied myself when I have a row with Mark? I proceeded to recite the list of his sins, chopping the edge of my right hand into the palm of my left to emphasize each one as I ground it through clenched teeth.

'You cause chaos, you embarrass me, you push me into being rude to someone who hasn't done anything wrong, and then you tell me that none of it's your fault because it was all an accident. Well, I'll tell you what *is* your fault. You don't *think*! That's your fault, isn't it? You're not aware of anybody else. If there's no chance of you gaining something personally from a situation then it's of no interest to you. It just doesn't exist!'

'That's nice – so that's what you think of me, is it?'

'Kathy, don't you think –'

I swung a warning finger in the direction of my husband.

'Just for once, Mike, *please*, just for *once*, could you let me have my say without interrupting and taking Mark's side?'

I turned back to my son, who was sitting very still now and studying the end of the table again.

'Would you like me to tell you, just as a matter of interest, how I always manage to find the comb that you have to borrow from me every morning because you lose every single one you ever have within about three minutes of getting it? *Would* you like me to do that?'

Silence.

'Well, would you?'

'Not partic'ly.'

'It is always in exactly the same place, Mark. In the middle of the hall carpet just under the place where the mirror's hanging, that's where I find my comb. And it's there because when you've finished doing your hair you just – drop it! I've stood and watched you lots of times. As soon as you think your hair looks okay, your fingers just open involuntarily and the comb drops out of them on to the floor. It doesn't exist any more, you see, because you've got no use for it. I'm very much afraid that's the way you tend to treat people as well, Mark, and you're going to have to do something about it, because when you leave here no-one's going to put up with it the way we do.'

'You always do this!' The words seemed to burst out of Mark. 'You always start saying things about my whole life when I do one thing wrong. You're always on about what I never do an' what I always do. You don't know me like you think you do. I only read a joke out and used the wrong spoon – that's all I did! You just look for reasons to say things to me, you do. I don't want any cereal now.'

Suddenly his lower lip started to tremble, just as it had done so often when he was a little boy. As his eyes filled with tears, he sent his huge bowl sliding down the table away from him and ran from the room, still clutching that ridiculous handkerchief of a towel around him.

Darkness filled me. I had made my son cry. Why? For what?

2

Mike sat down weakly on the chair that Mark had just vacated, shaking his head slowly in puzzlement. I turned round to the sink and loudly began the process of emptying the dishwasher and refilling it with last night's unwashed dinner things. I felt so ashamed and angry with myself. In recent weeks I had struggled more or less successfully to swallow the breathtaking fury that was periodically generated in me by Mark's behaviour, and now, in a few indulgent moments, I had blown it all completely and gone back to square one – no, probably the bit before square one, where you have to throw a compensatory six before you're allowed to get back on the board, let alone start moving again.

'Kath, have you decided what you're going to do about you and Felicity flying out to Pete and Dawn's later this year?'

I do so hate it when people try to *manage* me. I knew exactly what Mike was doing. Knowing full well that I was almost certainly inaccessible to reason and calm debate on the subject of what had just happened, he was making a wide conversational circle, a bit like those clever sheepdogs on television, with a view to penning me up good and tight when the right moment came. And he had chosen his route with care.

My older brother, Pete, adored by me since before time began, had emigrated to Australia with his wife fifteen years ago. I didn't think about my tall, dark, laughing, younger-sister-loving Pete all the time, of course, but every now and then a spasm of real pain would pass through me at the thought that I might never see him in the flesh again, and that my two attractive nieces were growing up in distant Brisbane without ever meeting an aunt whose ability to put people's backs up on a daily basis made a show like *Neighbours* look even blander than it actually was. I had always intended to use some of the money my mother left me to go out and see them, but you know how it is with money. It gets spent. This year, a week from now, in fact, I was to celebrate my fiftieth birthday, and, to my surprise Mike had suggested that a couple of thousand pounds, sitting in a building society account that Jack had shrewdly suggested we open a few years ago in readiness for when most of them went public and sprayed money around like a dung-spreader at planting time, should be used to fly Felicity and me off to the Antipodes for a family reunion.

Wonderful, eh? Yes, of course, but have you noticed the strange things that can happen when you're actually offered something you've always wanted? I've seen it on a much smaller scale the other way round, on those rare occasions when my sense of drama has fuelled an attempt to give substance to somebody else's casually expressed dream. At the moment when fantasy and reality touch there can sometimes be an effect like an electric shock. People don't like having their dreams messed with, perhaps because they offer a useful way to deal with reality.

In this connection I remember, a year or so ago, getting into trouble with Mike and our housegroup leader and just about everyone else except my friend Dip, when I asked someone a question on this very subject.

In our Bible study group we had a youngish couple (since moved on to pastures a little more explosively charismatic) called Bernard and Julie, who had been married for five or six years. Bernard, the husband, was a pleasant, laid-back sort of guy who drove a van around doing inexplicable things for the water board, and she was all right, I suppose, if a bit giggly and immature (not that I'm judging the foolish little person, of course). I think she had a job as a dental receptionist in one of the surgeries in our town, so perhaps having to witness all that fear and pain had affected her somehow.

Julie seemed to be wholly obsessed with Ralph Fiennes, about whom I knew only that he was a popular film actor. Whenever she talked about him, which was often and at length, she would go all droopy and languid and say how much she fancied him and dreamed about him and goodness knows what else. It really irritated me, I must admit, and her husband looked a bit browned off with it as well, although he never said anything in front of us. One evening, when we were all drinking coffee and stuff after the Bible study and Julie had somehow managed to wrench the conversation round from a discussion about which point in the service the notices should be given out to whether 'Ralph's' hair or mouth was his best feature, I asked her a perfectly innocent question – well, this is supposed to be a truthful account, so I confess that it wasn't that innocent, although I claimed it was at the time.

'Julie,' I said, 'can I ask you something about Ralph Fiennes?'

'Ooh, yes,' she dribbled, obviously a little surprised at my interest.

'You really fancy him, don't you?'

'Ooh, yes!'

'Well, suppose you had a phone call from him – from Ralph Fiennes, I mean – tomorrow morning, right?'

'Ooh, yes?'

'And he said, "Hi, there, Julie, I'll be round to your house at half past three to have wild sex with you," well, my question is – would you?'

The silence that followed this purely technical query was so profound that I began to think none of us would ever speak or move again. I wondered if we would just go on sitting there like actors in some frozen theatrical scene for the rest of time. It wasn't a very Bible-studyish question. Julie had turned bright scarlet, Mike had his I-thought-you'd-stopped-doing-things-like-that expression on his face, and most of the others just looked embarrassed. The only two who didn't were my dear friend Dip, who leaned her head right back so that she could study the ceiling, pressing her lips together to avoid smiling, and Bernard, who cocked his head in the direction of his wife as if keenly interested in hearing her answer to my question.

Mike was very chilly about it afterwards, and Simon Davenport, our housegroup leader, rang me up the following day to ask me how I felt about what I'd said. Translated, this was the crinkly-eyed, non-confrontational way of communicating the message, 'You shouldn't have said it', and I agreed with him in order to keep the peace.

Funny things, dreams.

And the Australian dream was a really tricky one. Part of me wanted nothing more than to jet off with Felicity to visit my brother and his family, but there was another cringingly immature part of me that was terrified of the actual meeting after all these years. What if I messed it up? What if the towering significance of the encounter shut down some part of my emotional confidence and made the whole thing uneasy and tense? I couldn't bear the thought of all my golden memories being transmuted into one leaden weight of failure. I found myself wishing that I was the sort of person who didn't think and ponder everything out of proportion so much, someone like Mike, who, when I made an attempt to explain my fears, looked utterly mystified, but nodded like a good counsellor and said, 'Just be yourself and I'm sure it'll all go fine.' I wanted to scream that it was 'myself' I was worried about.

'The answer to your question, Mike,' I replied, without turning round or ceasing my dishwasher operations, 'is that I intend to faff around, changing my mind repeatedly, until I'm faced with having to decide something, and then I shall make a random decision that will turn out to be wrong. I would have thought you knew that without having to ask. You know how consistent I am.'

There was a sigh from the other end of the kitchen. I felt sure that if I listened very hard it would be possible to hear Mike's brain thinking that there was no getting through to me when I was in this frame of mind. He tried again, though.

'So who was that on the phone earlier after all our messing about?'

Oh, God …

'Oh, yes, it was, err – it was Joscelyn. She wanted to tell me about her weekend away at that manor place, how much it ...'

'How it revolutionized her life in every particular, no doubt.'

There was a little chuckle in Mike's voice. He felt
himself to be on safe ground here. The business of
Joscelyn's need for epic spiritual adventures had
frequently been a topic of mild amusement and
genuine sympathy between us until now. He
continued with greater confidence.

'Well, that explains the earliness of the call. The
only reason I got fed up just now was that it was
your turn to look after everything and you kept
putting the phone down when I picked it up –
didn't you, you naughty person?'

Oh, no. Not the playful voice. Please, Mike,
don't start using the playful voice because you
think everything's sorting itself out. I always hate it
at the best of times, and especially now. Please, I
beg you, don't try to be playful ...

Running out of things to do with the washing-
up, I turned heavily to face my husband. I could
tell that he was feeling it wouldn't be very long
before we could safely move on to the subject of
Mark. A word more about Joscelyn first, though,
no doubt, just to round off that pleasant little chat.

'Hey, Kath, it's fortunate we know old Joss so
well, isn't it? If anyone else had phoned at that time
of the morning to talk about their spiritual condition I think you'd have told them where to go in no
uncertain terms, wouldn't you?'

It was impossible not to detect the extra question in his voice. Finding a hardened blob of some

ex-edible substance on the work-surface beside me,
I began to scratch at it with my thumbnail.

'I did.'

The light little laugh with which Mike had
concluded his last speech died an abrupt death at
the back of his throat. Feeling suddenly rather
weak at the knees I pulled out the chair at the other
end of the table and sat down. I waited for him to
run his hand through his hair and shake his head
as if to clear it. Having done both of those things he
spoke.

'What do you mean, you *did*?'

'I mean that I *did* tell Joscelyn where to go in no
uncertain terms – well, not exactly that, but, err ...'
I cleared my throat and looked up before going
on. 'You see, she was saying all the normal stuff
about – you know – everything changing, and I
was about to trot out all the usual affirming crap –
Mike, why do you always do that shooting-a-guilty-
look-towards-the-door thing when I say a word
you don't approve of? We're not smoking in the
toilets, you know. Or did you think there might be
an undercover Ofsted inspector hovering in the
hall, gathering evidence about the unsuitability of
your private life?'

'You know, you can be most unpleasant when
you're on the defensive,' said Mike in a very quiet
voice. 'I was just concerned that Felicity might have
come down and heard you talking like that, that's
all.'

'Well, she'd have had a job, seeing as she was at
Caroline Burton's sleep-over last night and hasn't

come home yet. Presumably this deep concern of yours for your ten-year-old daughter doesn't extend to a passing interest in where she might have spent the night.'

'What did you say to Joscelyn?'

'I can't believe that you'd really forgotten Felicity wasn't here. That seems extraordinary to me.'

Mike physically stretched himself back and away from my pathetic attempt to change the subject.

'Don't be silly. *What* did you say to Joscelyn?'

I steepled my fingers together and hid my face behind them.

'I told her that she never seems any different to me after these big God-binges of hers and that all she's really doing is getting nearer to finding out she's a sinner who's been saved.'

'Uh …'

Waves of irritated disapproval broke over my bowed head.

'And I, err – I told her that all her stuff about being completely transformed was a load of rubbish, and that what it boiled down to was her talking on and on about herself.'

'You said all that in those words?'

'No – yes – well, worse than that probably. I did say that I do it as well…'

I risked a glance over the palisade of my fingers. Judging by the expression on Mike's face I was about to be sent out into the corridor to do sums at a little table all day as an example to the other children. I remembered something else.

'Oh, and I finished by telling her that she needed to learn how to relax. Mmm, that's right, I did say that as well.'

'*You* criticized *her* for not being able to relax?'

'Yes.'

'I just don't know what to say …'

At these not infrequent moments when I openly confessed the enormity of my crimes I always had the feeling that Mike was silently and frustratedly urging me to tell *myself* off so that he wouldn't have to do it – smack my own face, as it were, and call myself names until I wept uncontrollably – and a little judicious comfort from him would be only right and proper. It maddened him that I spoke in a flattened voice and never automatically volunteered to scrub the latrines with a toothbrush or cut the lawn with nail-scissors as penance for my sins. Observing that, as usual, the hoped-for implosion of remorse was not on the cards, he moved on.

'And the girl at the door – the milkgirl – what did you say to her?'

'More or less told her to clear off because I didn't know what she was talking about and shut the door in her face.'

Mike was shaking his head again.

'Kath, I don't know how you can just sit there and say that so calmly as though it doesn't matter, I really don't.'

We are supposed to be Christians, you know.

'We are supposed to be Christians, you know.'

We sat in silence, Mike wondering why I didn't get on with the job of beating myself up, me

34

knowing wretchedly that we were about to move on to the subject that probably *would* make me cry.

'So, where does Mark come into all this, then? What did he do?'

I leaned back and slapped the palms of my hands down on my thighs, trying to remain brisk.

'I don't know.'

'You don't know what he did? Then why –'

'I know what I felt. I sort of know what he did. He didn't think.'

'About what?'

'Oh, Mike, you've heard me say it all before. You've heard me say it all before, before and before that. If I have to go through it all again I shall just end up sounding like a congenital idiot. The whole thing sounds so stupid. He wore a towel that was too small, he read a joke that wasn't funny, his towel fell off for half a nano-second, he was about to eat too many Shredded Wheat with too much sugar in the wrong-sized bowl using a giant spoon and, most reprehensible of all, he picked the wrong stupid mother. That's what happened.'

'And what was it about him dropping his – sorry, I mean *your* – comb on the hall carpet when he's finished with it? You seemed to feel that was a vitally important point.'

'Sarcasm doesn't become you, Mike. Why don't you just stick to being boring?'

Aaagh …!

I wanted to reach out with both hands and catch those last eight words I'd said before they could reach his ears. I couldn't, of course. You

never can, can you? They were said. They were
gone. They were doing whatever they would do.
Unable to stand the hurt and puzzlement in
Mike's eyes, I pushed my chair back and walked
round behind him so that I could put my face
next to his and wrap my arms around his chest.

'Look, don't take any notice of what I say, Mike.
I know I've been horrible. I hardly slept last night.
I should have asked you to get up this morning
instead of inflicting myself on everybody. I woke up
so many times, worrying and trying to make sense
of things ...'

'Trying to make sense of what?'

His voice was horribly cold.

'Oh, just *things* – stupid things. It's always the
same, everything seems so much more intense and
serious in the middle of the night, doesn't it? I just
got it all out of perspective. You know what I'm like
when I don't sleep – the wife and mother from
hell.'

My heart sank. There was something rigid and
unyielding about the feel of my husband's upper
body. Mike was a very kind man. Usually, any
mention of lack of sleep or a bad night was good for
a pat on the hand at the very least. Not now,
though. Carefully unwrapping my arms, he leaned
forward with his elbows on the table and spoke
without looking at me.

'One of the things you were trying to make sense
of all through the night was why you've ended up
married to someone as tedious as me, was it,
Kathy?'

I decided I owed him the truth.

'Mike, I don't want to be ...'

'What?'

'I'll tell you in a minute. Just – just let me do something first.'

Retrieving Mark's Brobdingnagian breakfast from the other end of the table, I carried it along the hall, opened the front door and baptized it in nearly a whole pint of the milk left by our recently extinguished lactic entrepreneur. When I presented this peace offering to Mark in his room a few moments later, he was somewhat taken aback, but very pleased and willing to accept it. A vast bowl of cereal in the hand is worth any amount of justified lingering resentments in the bush.

'Sorry about just now, Mum,' floated down the stairs after me as I descended.

'So am I.'

Same old pattern. Someone throws an apology into the ring, and someone else picks it up. Doesn't much matter who does which.

I got back to the kitchen to find Mike sitting exactly as I had left him, staring into space with an expression so sad and serious that it cut into me like a sharp knife. I sat next to him.

'Don't want to be what?' he asked very quietly, as if I'd never left the room.

'I don't want to be fifty,' I said, and burst into tears.

3

'So whose idea was this party?'

'It was Mike's idea, amazingly, Dip. He said we couldn't bring the old days back, but we might as well remind ourselves of what they were like by having a sixties party. I think it's a really good idea. And then he said he thought we ought to have it next Saturday, actually on my birthday, and I said a week's such short notice that people won't be able to come, but he said try them. So I got our little book out and phoned loads of people one after the other on the spot, and so far they've all said yes. And the following week's half-term, so we'll have a whole week to recover in. So, there we are – it's on! Exciting, eh?'

'What did you mean about it being amazing that it's Mike's idea?'

'Oh, well, what I mean is – it's amazing considering how he pretends to loathe big untidy things that make a mess. You know what he's like as well as I do.'

'I think it's a good idea, too,' chipped in Felicity, aged ten, taking her pen from between her teeth to speak. 'You'll be a twentieth of a thousand years old, Mummy. How many of my friends can I ask? Can we move the big telly up to Mark's room and have videos?'

It was early afternoon, and a sort of peace had once more descended on the Robinson household. One of the strange things about our lives is the way in which high drama and twiddly ordinariness seem to alternate quite naturally. At ten o'clock we could all be in deepest, darkest despair, but by eleven o'clock we might easily be laughing like drains, or shelling peas and discussing the price of kitchen-rolls. By the time Dip arrived at eleven o'clock, Felicity was back from Caroline's with a ludicrously excessive party-bag full of vile-looking sweets and colouring pens (Caroline's mother, Sally Burton, was having difficulty in understanding that her little girl was no longer six, and she had always been very competitive in this area, in any case), and Mark had gone off to his weekend job at the stationer's in the high street. Incredibly, Mike and I had progressed from near divorce to gooey cuddliness in about half an hour flat, and he had now driven off to eat a large lunch, play uncommonly guiltless golf and look forward to a little mild marital flirting with his repentant wife when he got back.

'What sort of things will you do at your party, Mummy? Food and talking and selling things nobody wants and that, all in a circle?'

We both sat in silence for a second, inwardly digesting Felicity's picture of the sort of party adults might enjoy.

'Certainly not, totally wrong, small and silly person,' I replied eventually. 'Your mummy is going to have the sort of party we had back in the sixties. The house will be jammed – stuffed with hordes of people who love me very much, all swirling around the house, listening to David Bowie records turned up too loud, and talking complete nonsense to each other about the meaning of life – that will be compulsory. And we're going to have a room where people pile their coats when they arrive and have trouble finding them at the end. What else, Dip?'

Dip looked at me slightly oddly for a moment, then dropped her eyes and rubbed the top of her head with the tips of her fingers as she spoke.

'Well, I suppose there'll have to be a place by the kitchen door where I can be trapped for the whole evening by a man with bad breath telling me in gory detail about all the awful things that are making his life miserable. It wouldn't be the sort of sixties party I remember if that didn't happen.'

'You're all weird,' pronounced Felicity. 'Can I go and ring Caroline?'

'You've been with her solidly since the beginning of yesterday evening. Which vitally important thing did you forget to say in the course of the last fourteen hours? Why do you need to ring her now?'

Eyes wide with concentration, Felicity tapped the end of her pen against her teeth as she tried to think of an answer.

'Tell her about the party, of course.'

'All right, clear your pens and paper up first, then.'

'I'm going to carry on afterwards, Mummy. There's no point putting it all away, is there?'

'All right, but if you don't carry on you will be severely punished. Go!'

'Can I do it from your room?'

'Go, will you!'

Dip laughed affectionately as my slim, golden-haired daughter twirled her way out through the door, pulling a silly face as she went.

'She's so lovely, isn't she? I used to wish she'd stay little, but I'm glad she hasn't.'

My heart was warmed all over again by the fond expression on my friend's face. Dip (real name Elizabeth Reynolds) had known Felicity since she was a baby, and probably loved her as much as we did. She was also my best friend, and very popular with the rest of the family, especially Mark, who seemed to find things he needed in her (acceptance being one trivial example) that he was seldom able to find in me. I confess that I had had to battle hard with resentment of that fact from time to time, but the better part of me was glad that she had been there for him over the last few years. She and I were very different in a number of ways. I was wild, she was mild. Everything about Dip was comfortable and comforting. No-one has ever described me as comfortable. I was dark, like my younger son, and a little over average height. She was a few years older than me, quite tall with short fair hair, gorgeous blue eyes and a slight but unmistakable Australian accent left over from her early life in Adelaide. She worked part-time as a nurse in the local hospital and belonged to the same church and housegroup as us. The areas we did have in common included an extremely silly sense of humour, a shameless attachment to the best sherry in the world, and a real passion for God. These three seemed to get us through most things.

41

A few years earlier we had decided as a family that we would all love to have Dip living with us. Just before flying off on holiday to America, we issued a ceremonial and absolutely definite invitation, then left her to look after our house and our two stick-insects, Rowan and Kimberley (long since departed to the great bramble-patch in the sky), while she attempted to make a decision about whether to move in permanently or not when we came back. We were all quite surprised when she announced that she'd decided to stay in her little terraced house on the other side of Standham, but when I saw later what she'd written about – well, about being *her*, I think I understood. Funny, isn't it? You really think you know people. (If you want to know where her nickname came from, by the way, I won't bother telling you now, because she's written all about that as well.)

'So, what started all this off, then, Kathy?'

Dip was continuing a conversation that had been interrupted and radically adjusted as a result of Felicity arriving in the living-room to commence her third unfinished activity of the morning since getting back from the Burtons' house.

'Well …'

'Suddenly realizing fifty is coming towards you like an express train and getting into a bit of a panic because evil, moustachio-twirling life has tied you to the tracks? That's more or less how it felt to me.'

'Yes, I think it's been – did you just make up that "moustachio-twirling life" bit, Dip, or did you have it all prepared? I bet you've been waiting ages for an opportunity to casually trot that out, haven't you?'

She threw her head back and laughed.

'I'm sorry. Is my conversation usually so boring that a sudden pathetic burst of metaphor calls for special celebration? If so, I'll have a small sherry.'

'I thought you'd never ask. As you know, we have a small bottle specially set aside for celebration of metaphor, in the grammatical section of the drinks cabinet.'

Two minutes later we both had a glass of Bristol Cream in our hands. I took a lovingly reverent sip and decided to answer Dip's question truthfully.

'Mike and I were invited out to dinner a few weeks ago by the Handleys, who live in one of those really huge Victorian houses in Swan Road, the ones with the long drives and lovely big sash windows that still work. You know the Handleys, don't you? I think she works up at the charity shop in the precinct most mornings, and Frank was something terribly important to do with the House of Commons before he retired, but not a member of parliament or anything. They used to go to our church, if you remember, then they retired and stopped coming for some reason, and Mike ran into Frank on a committee a couple of months ago and –'

Dip raised a hand in surrender.

'I know who you mean. I never knew them very well, but I *do* know who you mean.'

'Well, it doesn't really matter, actually. We never knew them very well either, that was the trouble. So we were both a bit stiff and nervous. Their *house!*' I lowered my voice as though the Handleys might be crouching behind the sofa listening to us. 'Dip, I've never seen anything like it. Huge place, all leather and polished wood and antiques and things made out of elephants' feet, and a lady who comes to "do" for them, you know the sort of thing I mean. I think Mike's just the tiniest bit susceptible to your genuine poshness –'

'Oh, me too, I'm afraid,' sighed Dip.

'And he goes into this funny sort of falsely relaxed mode, specially after a couple of drinks. It's difficult to describe – somewhere between senti-mentalism and spurious worldly wisdom. Drives me mad, because he usually calls on me to support his attempted witticisms or tinny little scraps of home-spun philosophy and all I want to do is tell him to shut up.'

'But you don't?'

'No, of course I don't, not if I can help it, but with the Handleys I came very close to it. After dinner we got on to the subject of "marriage in this day and age", and you know how it is at dinner parties with people you don't know very well. Somehow you get carried away on a wave of enthu-siastic agreement about absolutely everything in the universe because it's too much like hard work if you don't, and after a while you hear yourself talking absolute piffle or saying things you don't actually go along with at all, and your brain goes all numb and dead and you just want to go home and die of shame. Anyway, we'd all solemnly agreed that young couples nowadays don't have the moral fibre that young couples used to have, and that "commitment" was a word people don't seem to understand nowadays, by Jove, and that in our day (their day was considerably before our day, I might point out, but we were good enough or cowardly enough not to remind them of that) you made your promises and *damn well stuck to them* through thick and thin, and all that stuff, and then Frank whatever-his-name-is said what he thought the real trouble was. The *real* trouble, he declared, was that the youngsters of today expected fireworks (meaningful nod to indicate that he was speaking of "marital unpleasantness", as that character of Harry Enfield's calls it) all the way in their marriages, and gave up when it didn't happen. Surely, he inquired confidently, Mike would agree with him that such expectations were ridiculous.

'That was when Mike embarked on one of those little speeches of his that sceptics like us might suspect are designed to snuggle up to the good opinion of people he feels inferior to. They make my bones ache! Dip, it wouldn't have mattered if he'd just nodded and grunted something or other that sounded like a vague agreement – I mean, I don't really care what the posh Handleys think about our sex-life – but he didn't.

'"No," said the style-king of the junior teaching world, the Oscar Wilde of Standham, swirling the brandy round in his glass and sipping with judicious consideration. "I don't think you could describe what happens in a mature relationship as

45

fireworks. No, Frank, I would say that long-term marriage is more like one of those wonderful, heavy old Aga cookers – wouldn't you agree, Kathy? They last for years if you look after them properly, it's possible to get a really excellent glow going, and they produce really good meals as long as you give 'em a stoke every now and then." Dip, this sherry is very expensive. If you're going to spit it all over the room I shan't give you any next time.'

'I'm sorry!' spluttered Dip, 'I really am. Give me some more. Gosh, I bet he wished he hadn't said that afterwards.'

'Oh, yes, afterwards, you may bet your best cami-knickers on it. At the time, though, he just sat back and lapped up all the expensive, throaty sounds of merriment from Frank and Thingy Pooey Poshperson. Then, in the car on the way home, he said it had really gone well, didn't I think? And I said, using my famous impression of a cucumber served after twenty-four hours in the freezer, "I regret to announce that the heavy old Aga has gone out through consistent neglect and will require a complete service before it becomes functional again. Because of this there will certainly be no glowing tonight, and you need not expect any really good meals in the foreseeable future, stoke every now and then though you may," and it was then that he began to realize I wasn't too impressed with his little flash of wit. Actually, we did laugh about it next morning, but ...'

'But it set you thinking.'

'It was a sort of trigger, I suppose, Dip. I started to feel very sad, and worried and panicky about getting old and everything winding down and feeling flat. I don't *want* to be a heavy old Aga that glows sometimes. I'm not interested in being one of those highly respected Christian women in suits, with kind-sad eyes, who resisted temptation once for all the very best reasons and are in a sensible long-term relationship with no fireworks and have written a Lent book about it. I want some sparklers and some bangers and some rockets and some – some things you have to be very careful with because they could be dangerous. There's got to be at least an outside chance of getting your fingers burned, hasn't there?' I paused, sipping my sherry again and wondering how much more to say. 'I started to feel as if there was a really big decision to be made.'

'About what?'

'Well, at the risk of you thinking I've finally looped the loop, it was – well, I saw it like this. It was the decision about whether to burst like an exploding star, or shape myself like a comfortable armchair. I didn't feel ready to get old and spend my time shaping myself into whatever other people wanted me to be. I really didn't want that. I wanted lots of other things. I wanted to go through those first stages of falling in love again, Dip, when you go for a walk and ordinary things like trees and buses and brick walls look shiny and vivid and textured and full of meaning. Do you remember that glorious, half-witted feeling?'

'I remember –'

'I wanted to turn up in some cafe on Saturday morning at ten thirty with everything in me buzzing and tingling because I was going to meet someone I'd been dreaming about all night and dressing and making-up for since getting up. I wanted to walk along a river-bank under weeping willows in the autumn like Mike and I used to when we first discovered each other up at Durham, finding to our amazement, like all couples falling in love since the beginning of time, that we felt exactly the same about absolutely everything under the sun, wondering when it would be right to hold hands for the first time, and whether he would kiss me when we got back to the halls, and worrying about not being able to do it properly and – and all those warm and fruity things. I sat up really late in the kitchen one hot summer night this year with all the doors open, feeling one of those magical warm breezes running right through the length of the house from front to back, just gently brushing my face. It was sad and lovely, and it filled me full of aching and longing for – for something or other. Do you know – ?'

I looked at my friend for a moment. How safe is it to say some things?

'Go on,' said Dip, 'you might as well spit it out.'

'In case it's infected, you mean? Sorry. Sorry, it's just that I was embarrassed for a moment. It seems so ridiculous to be saying this sitting at home on a Saturday morning at eleven o'clock – but there've been times when I wanted to sneak off down to a pub in the next town and sit at the bar and have a couple of drinks and see if I got chatted up.'

'That doesn't sound much like the "wondering when it would be right to hold hands" sort of stuff that you were talking about.'

Putting my glass down on the small table beside me, I clasped my hands tightly together as I tried to find the words to explain.

'Oh Dip, it wasn't that I really did want some sordid encounter with a fifth-rate gigolo from Milton Keynes – always assuming there might be a fifth-rate gigolo in Milton Keynes who specializes in travelling down this way for sordid encounters with forty-nine-year-old mothers of three. And I'm not one for getting crushes on film stars, like that droopy girl we used to have in our group.' I couldn't help laughing suddenly. 'Honestly, Dip, can you imagine me taking on the role of resident *femme fatale* in the Dog and Duck on Friday nights? It isn't just about sex, you see, Mike and I have always got on pretty well in that area – well, most of the time, anyway – it's more about feeling special and sparkly and – and fancied. Do you know what I mean?'

'Well, I …'

I think I did actually notice out of the corner of my mind, as it were, that Dip was looking a trifle strained or strange or something by this point, but I ploughed on without waiting for a reply, as I'm afraid I so often do with my close friends, and especially this one, oblivious to any universe but the one existing solely for the benefit of Kathy Robinson.

'So, after I'd accused Mike of being boring this morning, and then admitted that my real fear was getting old and him thinking I was boring, it was like a boil bursting – no, that's horrible, it wasn't like that. It was like a bubble popping – no, as you were, it was definitely a boil. Anyway, whatever it was, bubble or boil, it burst, and after that we got more glutinously lovey-dovey than we've managed to be at that passionless time of the morning for ages. And Mike said why don't we celebrate the beginning of me being old by having a real old-fashioned sixties party with the right music and silly dancing in tiny spaces because the room is too crowded and all the other things we were talking about just now. And he has promised, a little worriedly, him being stuck with being who he is, that he will do his best to ensure that romance will blossom once again in our relationship. In the meantime, I have to repair the damage I've done to our friendship with Joscelyn, apologize to the girl who delivers the milk, and be pro-actively nice to Mark to make up for this morning. I must say, you know, Dip, with the best will in the world, there is nothing like three children for killing the prospect of careless and spontaneous passion in a marriage. Sometimes I wish they would all clear off somewhere and be happy. So, there we are! That's my day so far. What do you think?'

I didn't know what Dip was going to reply to this, but whatever it was had no chance of being heard, because Felicity reappeared at that moment clutching a sheet of paper in her hand. Smiling a funny little frowning smile and signalling that she was just popping out to the hall for a moment, Dip slipped through the open door.

'Mummy, I've got a question for you. Which is the most frightening prehistoric monster of all, more frightening than tyrannosaurus rex or raptors, or any of those in the film you wouldn't let me see and Daddy did? Jack just wrote it down for me.'

Felicity was indeed once more among us, bright with her interest in whatever it was she wanted to communicate. Jack was her oldest brother, just back from his final term at university and working through one of the local job agencies during the week, while he considered the little matter of what to do with the rest of his life. Jack never seemed to get out of his bed unless there was some exception-ally good reason for doing so. Today was Saturday and there was not even a bad reason for surfacing. No doubt his little sister had jumped on him, ignored his groans and demanded entertainment. Their relationship was a constant joy to me. I had been so afraid that when Jack went away Felicity would lose touch with the feeling of closeness there had been between them for the first few years of her life. Not a sign of it.

'Go on, then,' I said, 'let's hear it.'

'Okay.' She cleared her throat and read from her piece of paper. ' "The most frightening dinosaur of all is one that has not become extinct like all the other dinosaurs, but can still be found in this present age, lurking in libraries, studies and bookshops all over England. It is called the Thesaurus, and it is huge, massive, very large, enormous, gar – gargantuan, colossal, king-size, monstrous, immense, titanic and vast. Because of this, anyone who sees, observes, spots, notices, views, perceives, regards, witnesses or looks at it, is likely to be terrified, aghast, petrified, scared, shocked, alarmed and windy." *Windy*!' she repeated with a peal of laughter, 'I think I'd be windy if I saw a dinosaur. Maybe that would put it off eating me.'

'Well, it would me. Just as a matter of interest, darling daughter,' I said, 'do you know what a thesaurus really is?'

'Yes, Mummy,' she replied calmly, referring once more to her sheet of paper, 'it is a collection of concepts or words arranged according to sense. What did you think it was?' She grinned. 'Jack said you'd ask me that.'

'I shall come up those stairs in a minute and make your lazy big brother swallow Mr Roget's entire collection of concepts or words arranged according to whatever you said in a minute. You go and tell him that, and tell him to get up and come down and say hello to Dip.'

'I think Dip's gone, Mummy,' said Felicity. 'I just heard the front door go.'

'What? What are you talking about? No she hasn't, she's just gone out to the – the toilet or something.'

I got up quickly and went into the hall. No sign of anyone there. Calling up the stairs brought no response either. Opening the front door I walked as far as the gate and, leaning over, looked up and down our road, expecting to be met with the familiar sight of Dip's elderly but beloved Mini, Daffodil. There were lots of places available for cars to be left, including the space under the tree directly outside our house where she usually parked, but the Mini simply wasn't there. Felicity was right. Dip had gone.

4

That sort of thing has an odd effect on the pit of your stomach, doesn't it? I may be wrong to think this applies to lots of people, but I have always supposed that one of the security blankets most of us cling to is the knowledge that, in nearly all respects, we are battling through the same things together in this wild world. And, if you're anything like me, it tends to be the common understanding and close identification possible through truly close friendships that are the most secure things of all. If you like, you and your friend are facing the same way to withstand the onslaught, shoulder to shoulder, which, in my view, is the most matey configuration of all.

I'm really beginning to wish I hadn't vowed to be totally truthful in this account. You're going to think I'm hopelessly egocentric – well, I expect you do already, but even more so, I mean – when I tell you that Dip's disappearance left me feeling almost breathlessly lost and hurt. It was as though she and I had escaped from a sinking ship by clambering on to the same little life raft, and suddenly, after a long experience of clinging together in order to survive, she had unaccountably slipped away into the water and left me on my own. Ridiculous! She'd only gone out of the house – once! – without saying goodbye. It was hardly on a par with the *Titanic* tragedy.

But why? *Why?* Why had she? I went back to the kitchen and sank into a chair, head in hands, trying to make sense of what had happened. Why had Dip gone? She just didn't do that sort of thing. She simply did not get up from her seat, walk out of the front door, and drive away without looking back or saying goodbye, or telling anyone, or – or anything. I cast my mind back as best I could over the conversation we had just had, searching for a clue that might help to solve the mystery of such unusual behaviour. I had certainly talked a lot and not done much listening, but that was hardly unusual. And anyway, Dip was never backward about telling me what she thought about that aspect of my personality.

There had been the time, for instance, when a family court found me guilty of continually trying to control everybody and everything around me. They cited such family events as Chinese meals when, according to them, the tedious process of individual decision-making made me so irritable that I always attempted to whip or bludgeon everyone into ordering one of the set meals for five so that we and they could 'get on with it'. Somewhat bruised by them painting this picture of me as a sort of impatient bully, I had appealed to Dip when she joined us a little later.

'Dip,' I said, 'they're all accusing me of being controlling over things like meals and trips and that sort of thing. Would you say I was the kind of person who tried to control other people? Don't be polite, be honest.'

'Oh, yes,' replied Dip pleasantly and casually, 'that's exactly how you are.'

I hesitate to record yet more evidence of my need to be confined in a place with nice soft walls where I can't easily hurt myself, but as the reality of Dip's abrupt departure started to sink in, I even began to feel a faint shadow of dread that was a little bit similar to the sort of fear I had known as a slightly younger child than Felicity was now, when a visiting preacher at my parents' church had talked with loud and cheap-suited authority about 'The Rapture'. This harbinger of peace and joy had described how two people would be working in a field and one would be snatched up and go off to be with God, while the other would be left on his or her own. He claimed that one airline in the state of California had instituted a rule that, of the pilot and co-pilot who crewed their planes, at least one must not be a born-again Christian, in case both were taken by God and the plane crashed. I listened goggle-eyed and was terrified! I remember reef-knotting myself to my mother's arm on the way home, hoping that, if this rapture business happened before we reached the solidly roofed safety of our house, I would be hooked up into the sky on her arm, and God would let me stick around because it was so obvious how much my mother loved and would miss me if I stayed on earth and she lived in heaven. It took me a long time to get over that sermon.

I comforted myself with the reflection that yellow Minis were unlikely to be included in God's rapturous removal plans.

Nevertheless, by the time Jack made his yawning entrance into the kitchen a few minutes later, I had managed to get myself into a bit of a state. He stopped on his well-worn path to the kettle and studied me expertly for a moment.

'Coffee and counselling, Mumsy?'

'Hello, Jack, darling. Yes, I'll have a coffee, thanks. No counselling needed, though. I don't suffer from a mysterious and unaccountable reluctance to walk out in front of moving buses, nor am I trying to control an unnatural urge to attack Labour politicians with cactuses wrapped in cling-film.'

'Oh, dear, bad as that, eh? Where's Dad? It's cacti, by the way.'

'I don't care what it is – incorrect plurals are the least of my problems at the moment. Golf. What do you mean – bad as that?'

'Well,' said Jack calmly, filling the kettle from the tap and plugging it in as he spoke, 'as I've explained to you before at some length, ever since I was a small boy you've set out to entertain me when something's wrong, instead of simply telling me what's up. It's supposed to put me off, and it used to, but now that I'm incredibly mature I see through it immediately, so it's a waste of time.' He perched himself on the stool by the sink and held out a tin towards me. 'Biscuit?'

'No thanks, but, err, I would like to have that coffee you've offered me. Is there any chance that the full power of your incredible maturity could be focused on to the need to actually switch the kettle *on* so that the water has a chance to become hot enough to make it? What's Felicity doing? She needs to do a violin practice today.'

'Oh, yeah! Sorry, it's on now. Writing out a news bulletin for later, that I suggested. She's all right. What's happened? You're upset. Tell Uncle Jack.'

It said a lot for the way things had changed that I proceeded to do exactly that.

One day, at about the age of nineteen, Jack had favoured Mike and me with what you might call a comprehensive run-down on ways in which the 'Enid Blyton' boy he accused us of trying to create had run into great difficulties when faced with the grittily real world of teenage life in general and secondary education specifically. He also said some gratifyingly nice things about us, thank God, and this highly emotional encounter turned out to be most constructive in the long run. One crucial item in Jack's complaint package had been his feeling that we tried to shield him from family issues and problems that might worry or upset him. He made it abundantly clear that he would rather unite with us in facing trouble, whatever it might be, than hear about it by accident and be more upset than if he'd heard about it in the first place. Being a simple soul in some ways, it had been quite hard for poor old Mike to hear any of the things that his oldest son so needed to express, and especially difficult to make this particular adjustment. You will not be surprised to hear that it was relatively easy for me, since running off at the mouth happens to be a bit of a speciality of mine.

Nevertheless, as I looked at the tall, lean figure of my son, draped on the stool in front of me, I found it difficult to believe that he was very nearly twenty-four, and quite definitely an adult who happened to live in the same house as us.

As Jack finished making our coffee I explained about everything that had happened that morning, with just a little judicious editing of the comments I had made about myself (for my own benefit rather than his), finishing with an expression of my real puzzlement about Dip's vanishing so unexpectedly and completely.

'The thing is,' I said, 'it's such a very definite – oh, what's the word? You know – what's the very definite thing that people make in books? Something vaguely unpleasant to do with banks, is it?'

'A definite statement?' suggested Jack.

'Yes, that's it – such a very definite statement. "I have removed myself without any reference to you." What's a person saying when they do something as unusual and total as that? It reminds me of when my mother – when Nanna died.'

There was a pause, then Jack spoke.

'Look, Mum, there's a couch in the next room where you can lie down, and I've got a false beard and a notebook and pencil and an old pair of horn-rimmed glasses upstairs. We might as well do this thing properly.'

Why does Jack's mickey-taking draw me in a way that sympathy pure and simple rarely does?

'No, I mean it. Mixed up in all the upsetness and crying and missing her there was quite a lot of hurt and bewilderment about her being able to just go so completely when she was supposed to love me so much. Please don't bother to tell me that's not rational. I know it doesn't make any sense – but then, what does?'

I stopped and thought for a moment.

'You know, I had a dream about my mother a couple of years after she died that I never told anyone about, not even Dad. It really upset me at the time.'

Sigmund Robinson detached himself from his stool and sat at the opposite end of the table. He took the elastic band from his pony-tail and, keeping his eyes fixed on me, began to readjust it.

'Go on, then, Mumsy. Hit me with the bad dream.'

'Well, I was in Grantley – you know, her village – walking along the high street with the shops and houses and all that as normal. It wasn't in the past – I mean, in my dream she'd died and everything, and I was just there, feeling sad. And then, quite suddenly, *there she was*, crossing the road in front of me. I could only see her back, but – you remember Nanna's shape, don't you, the sort of triangle her back made – it couldn't have been anyone else. I was so excited and pleased. I hurried to overtake her but when I caught her up and turned to look her in the face, she – oh, Jack, her eyes were a long, long way away, and they were – bruised with deadness. I so wanted her to give up being dead and come back and make everything how it used to be. Then, in my dream, I looked down and saw that her big, old-fashioned knickers had fallen down round her feet, so I told her and she started to bend down as though she was going to pull them up, but she stopped almost immediately and looked at me, all sad and helpless, and – and somehow I knew she'd stopped because there's no point in pulling your knickers up when you're dead. I felt like crying. I wanted to beg her to pull her pants up, just as a little sign that if she could have chosen she would have wanted to stay alive and walk along to the house I grew up in and have a cup of tea in the warm world with me, but her eyes were – so, so far away. Then I woke up, thank God.'

I shivered suddenly in the warm kitchen. Jack wiped his eyes with the knuckles of one hand, then looked up.

'Dip's not dead, Mum.'

'No, I know. I'm being silly. What happened with her was just like a kind of echo, I suppose. I can't believe I'm so feeble.' I stood up. 'Perhaps if I give her a ring it'll turn out to be some really ordinary thing that she suddenly remembered and rushed off to do, and we'll both have a good laugh and it'll be all right.'

'Mum, why did Dip come round this morning?'

I sat down again.

'Why did she come round?' I gazed blankly at him for a moment. 'Why does she ever come round? To see us – have a cup of coffee, glass of sherry, bit of a chat. What are you getting at?'

'This morning in particular – I just wondered if there was anything special about her coming.'

I put my hand to my mouth like a child caught telling fibs.

'Actually, I think she did say yesterday she wanted to come and talk about something important, and I did rather go on and on and on about the trials and tribulations of being me and – and fifty and everything. But that still doesn't really explain – does it? Surely not.'

Jack shrugged. 'Depends what the important thing was, I suppose. Why don't you ring her?'

I stood up again.

'I will, I'll ring her now.'

I collided with Felicity in the doorway. She put her arms lovingly around me and looked soulfully into my face.

'Mummy, you and Daddy owe me two pounds, thirty-nine pence.'

I looked soulfully back at her.

'Felicity, for ten years we have clothed you, fed you, paid for your outings, furnished and equipped your room, taken you on holiday and financed your vast range of after-school activities.

Help me to understand how we can possibly have ended up owing *you* two pounds, thirty-nine pence.'

'You just do,' said my daughter sweetly, quite unmoved by this very cogent argument. 'Daddy said yesterday. Why did Dip go?'

'I don't know, but I'm going to find out. Take it out of my purse on the dresser. I'm just going to make a call from upstairs. Jack, can you make sure I'm not interrupted, please?'

'Do you want to hear our news bulletin, Mummy?'

'I'd love to later, sweetheart, but I must phone Dip to make sure she's all right. Okay?'

'Don't worry, Mummy, I'm going round the corner to the shop. Give Dip my love. Coming, Jack?'

Jack pushed himself out of his chair and drained his mug.

'Okay, Flitty, good idea. We might meet some of your friends and I can sing to them.'

'Promise you won't.'

'I might dance as well.'

'I don't want you to come now.'

'Oh, I'm coming all right …'

The sound of good-natured banter drifted away as I went up the stairs and they set off for the shops. I sat on the edge of the bed, watching through the window of our room for a minute or two as they dawdled and danced their way along the pavement. Those were two of my children there. My children. They looked all right, didn't they? Fit –

laughing. I'd brought them up – well, helped to bring them up.

I tried to summon up the nerve to ring Dip. The fluttery feeling in my stomach took a little while to calm down, but at last I picked up the receiver and dialled the familiar six-figure number. After five rings the cowardly part of me began to hope there would be no reply. I decided to let it ring another four times before hanging up. At least then I wouldn't have to feel guilty about not having tried hard enough. It wasn't, I told myself, that I didn't want to make contact with Dip, it was just that I had no idea what to expect, and I have always feared black surprises like other people fear spiders.

On the fourth ring there was a crackling and clicking at the other end, as though someone had done something, but still there was no voice to be heard. My own voice sounded husky and strained with tension as I spoke.

'Hello, could I speak to Dip, please?'

It was an absurd thing to say. I don't know who I thought I might be speaking to if it wasn't Dip. She lived on her own, and I could imagine nothing but the most extreme circumstance in which anyone else would answer her phone. There was a pause of a few seconds, then Dip's voice, slow, slightly blurred, but unmistakably hers, spoke dully and as if from a distance.

'Something you forgot to moan about, was there?'

'Dip, you sound funny, I can hardly hear you.'

'I'm speaking on the – when you don't – you know – you don't have to pick it up. Did you say you can hardly hear me? Oh – well, that's fine then, isn't it? That's fine. *I* can hear *you*, so that's fine. No change there, eh? That is ab-so-bloody-lute-ly fine!'

'Dip, you're – you're a bit drunk. You don't get drunk. You've got drunk without me.'

'Oh, Miss Marple strikes again! Do I remind you of some sad old single biddy in the village who overdosed on cough medicine? Yes, Katherine, I am somewhat intoxicated. I am – I am an intoxicated Anglican of Antipodean extract – actually, perhaps I'm not, 'cause I can say that – but, look – I really cannot listen to *any* more of your incessant *moaning*, Katherine, I really cannot listen to ...'

'Dip, I was very selfish this morning. I never even asked you what it was you wanted to talk to me about. I'm sorry, I honestly am.'

'Huh! You honestly am, am I?'

'No, *I* am. *I* am very sorry, Dip. Dip, you sound like a stage drunk. What have you been drinking?'

'Damnation to myself – and some Scotch, and a few tablets.'

Oh, sweet Jesus, hold her until I can ...

'Dip, what did you want to talk to me about this morning? Please, *please* tell me. I really do want to know. I know I went on and on and on without listening, but this time I'm not going to. Take your time and just tell me. I'm listening. I *am* listening now. Give me another chance.'

Silence.

'I was so very young, you know – silly and young, I was.'

Pause.

'Kathy?'

'Yes, I'm here.'

'Kathy, I was only sixteen – that's all I was. I didn't even know…'

'What?'

'You know – who, what, how, when – nothing! I knew nothing!'

'Dip, are you talking about sex?'

'Huh! That may be what you call it. That may be what you call it, Mrs "Mike and I have always got on very well in that area" Robinson. D'you want to know what I call it? I call it something ugly happening in the dark among some smelly coats like you're going to have at your party when I was too drunk to know what was happening because some – some *man* had made me drink vodka or something and I'd never drunk anything like that before.'

Suddenly Dip's voice rose into a wail of sheer anguish. I gripped the phone tightly with both hands, my own eyes wet with tears, wanting so much to be there with her.

'I call it not even remembering it and never doing it again because I felt so sick and mucky and *bad*! Oh, Kathy …!'

Lord Jesus, please sit beside me on this bed and put your arm round my shoulders and whisper in my ear the words I should say to my friend. Forgive me for being so grumpy and rotten this morning and thank you for all my family and all the other things I'm so lucky to have. I expect I'll make all the same mistakes again tomorrow, but I'll try not to. I really will try…

'Dip, do you want me to come round? I can come straight away. Felicity's with Jack, so –'

Dip interrupted, her voice more under control now, but wobbly and faint with crying, more strongly Australian than I could remember ever hearing it before.

'Every single time I see her, Kathy – just about every single time I see that lovely, lovely girl of yours – it crashes against my chest. Boom! It crashes against my chest every single time I see your Fli – Fli – Felicity. It hurts so much, Kathy, and it won't go away.'

I covered my eyes with my left hand, looking for the least spot of light in the darkness. What on earth was she talking about? Crashes against … I asked the question as gently as I could.

'What is it that's hurting you, Dip? Just that – that it happened, or –'

'It's this heavy weight, Kathy, the one that got hung round my neck, the one I hung round my neck – so heavy – it hurts so much. I can't get rid of it, Kathy.'

She was pregnant. She had an abortion.

'Did you have to have it terminated, Dip?'

'No, not terminated – wrong word altogether. Don't say that. Killed. Killed is the word. That's the word. *Killed.* Had to have it done. My dad said it was the only way. Mum cried and flibbered about a bit, but she always did what he said. Our house wouldn't stop being shivery and dark because his – his bloody shame went roaming and roaring round and round outside like a monster, blocking out the light. It was huge, Kathy, so much bigger than – than what they killed. The thing they killed wasn't much bigger than a – a grain of rice, a little tiny grain of rice. Little tiny …'

She gave it a name.

'Dip, darling, did you give the – the baby a name?'

Silence. A small voice.

'How did you know?'

'Err, I didn't – really. What – what was the name?'

'Kathy, I've never said it out loud before. I've never dared.'

As I waited, Jack and Felicity came back into view up the road at the corner of the street. She was holding a bulging paper bag, probably filled with the familiar assortment of cheap sweets that I'd always said I'd never let my children eat. A cherry bootlace hung from her mouth, the sort that gets shorter and shorter as you walk and chew. Felicity's face was tilted up towards her brother in rapt attention, her features splitting continually into a wide grin at the things he said. I pictured Mark, fortified by the Shredded Wheat swamp he had carted into his system earlier, joking with customers up at the shop as he dispensed newspapers, stationery and postage stamps in his own inimitable style. He was very good with people, a darn sight better than me. I suddenly wanted to rush up there and throw my arms round him and tell him I loved him. He'd hate that. Jack, Mark and Felicity. Three names, and three whole people to go with them. Riches. Treasure.

'He – he's called David. I mean – I don't know whether he would have been a boy or a girl, but – but I've always called him David.'

Dip didn't sound quite so drunk any more, just tired and burdened and sad.

'The guilt's been terrible, Kathy – terrible, like a great lump of concrete or something, always there, always reminding me that he could have grown up, he could have learned to walk, and he could have run and jumped and fallen over and grazed his knee and cried and I could have kissed it and put something on it to make it better. But I didn't make it better – all I did was kill him, Kathy. I killed my little David.'

Dip started to cry again, but in a different way. When I told Mike about it later I said that the sound of that weeping seemed to me like a lake or sea of grief that had at last found a way to escape and flow evenly out of the place where it had been trapped for all those hard years.

We could have a communion service.

'Dip, I wonder if we should – look, if I put the phone down right now and drive round to you, are you going to be okay until I get there?'

'Yes.' Sniff. 'Yes, come round – don't worry, I'm not going to do anything silly. Just cry.'

'Sure?'

'Sure.'

'Felicity sends her love, by the way. See you in a jiff.'

5

The story that Dip haltingly related to me after a quite lengthy recovery period, as we sat drinking black coffee together in her little kitchen, was far from being an uncommon one, but no less tragic for all that. As a naive and inexperienced sixteen-year-old she had gone with a schoolfriend to a party in a different suburb of Adelaide from her own and been offered alcohol for the first time in her rather sheltered life. The fumbling act of procreation that followed was conducted in a panic-stricken haze among jackets and coats and scarves on one of the beds upstairs, and it had left Dip trembling with disgust and self-loathing which, over the following weeks, was transmuted into terror as she realized that she was almost certainly pregnant. A reasonably happy if tentative life was turned overnight into the traditional bad dream, made worse by the fact that she never woke up from it (except when she was asleep, as it were), and that her mother and father were solidly present in the nightmare with her. The moment when she told them of her pregnancy had closely rivalled that dismally loveless encounter at the party as the most appalling experience of her life.

'After I'd said this awful set of words I'd been dreading to hear coming out of my own mouth, my father just – I don't know how to put it – he sort of ejected out of his chair as though he'd been shot, or as if something had stung him really hard, and I remember the momentum of it carried him over to the window, and he just stood there stiffly with his back to me staring out at the traffic going past and saying nothing. Mum turned pale and went into one of her pronoun frenzies. "Who? What? Where? Why? When?" Then she started to cry. It was such a weird feeling, Kathy. I remember thinking to myself, "This is real life, but like a film. In a minute, Dad's going to turn around and ask me if I'm sure, and I'm going to tell him that I am, and then he's going to ask who the father is, and I'm going to have to say that I don't know, I don't remember, and he's going to be disgusted and appalled." He was always either disgusted or appalled, or, on special occasions like this, disgusted and appalled at all sorts of things. When I was a little girl I used to believe that the two words must have very specifically different definitions. Do you know what I mean?'

I nodded energetically.

'Yes, as a matter of fact, Jack and Mike and I were talking about that the other evening. We were saying that it's like when some great global disaster happens, and world leaders have to issue statements, but there's a problem because they all like to say something different, and there's only a few suitable words you can use. So you get the first one being "shocked, horrified and saddened" by the tragedy, whereas the next one's "appalled, alarmed and deeply sympathetic to the victims", if there are any. Then the third leader gets greedy and says he's "stunned, outraged, scandalized, sickened, aghast *and* disgusted", so by the time the fourth one gets out of bed late on the other side of the world after oversleeping, there's not much left to choose from, and he ends up informing the world that what has happened is "very unpleasant and really not very nice at all". Sorry … I'm blithering on as usual. So, were you right? Was your father disgusted *and* appalled?'

Dip had smiled a watery smile at my nonsense, but now she nodded sadly.

'Oh, goodness me, yes, he was. Several other things as well, I'm sure, but I can't recall what they were. I think the thing that hurt me most, although I know I wouldn't have been able to put it into words at the time, was the feeling that we were talking about something I'd brought on myself because of deciding to be "dirty" or immoral. Kathy, what happened at that party was nothing to do with sex at all, really. It was about a child – me – getting into a situation she didn't understand, and ending up being quite badly hurt. If I'd been run over by a car or something or fallen down some steps, Mum would have been all sympathy, and even Dad would have hovered uneasily around squeezing out grunts of formal compassion. That was what I needed when I told them. I felt like a six-year-old who's having a rotten time, and I just wanted to be cuddled and loved and told that everything would be all right in the end. I know it was a shock for them, and I can understand that much better nowadays, of course, but I was so scared and unhappy.'

Dip began to cry softly again. I made more coffee. After a little while she dried her eyes and went on to tell me how her father's insistence on dealing with the situation in a way 'satisfactory to all concerned' had proved too much for the fragile sixteen-year-old's instinctive belief that even an unwanted life is sacred. There was a termination. For the second time in a short while things were done to the young girl's body without the consent of her inner will, this time in the name of discretion and good sense, but from that day to this, Dip had only ever known real peace through distraction. In her mind, the hypothetical David, unborn but always sadly and accusingly present, had been waiting for forty years to hear her explain why his life had needed to end before it ever had a chance to begin.

In the preceding week, a week which included the anniversary of the abortion, Dip had reached a point of such unbearable tension and anguish that she had decided to open her pain up to someone at last, the someone being me. I cringed inwardly as I thought back over the content of my prattling comments earlier that day. I had said something about wishing my children would go away and be happy somewhere. I had said how much I wanted to experience those feelings of being in love again – being fancied. I gathered from poor Dip that, apart from a life-long devotion to Paul Newman and, rather interestingly, ornate fantasies about good-looking men encountered at the centre of complicated garden mazes (takes all sorts!), she had closed the door on the prospect of actually experiencing any of these things since the age of sixteen.

'Dip,' I said sadly, 'when I ranted on and on and on about my lot not being a happy one, you must have really wanted to hit me.'

'Yes, one in the kisser would have been nice – either that, or I'd have enjoyed running off with your splendid husband so that you'd have had to spend a few Fridays down at the Dog and Duck looking for another brave volunteer from Milton Keynes to take his place. You know, I think Mike's the only man I've ever really trusted.' She shifted uneasily in her chair. 'Kathy, I really am ever so sorry about all this. I usually manage to keep this sort of stuff to myself. In fact, I've become a bit of an expert at it. I just suddenly couldn't handle it any more this morning and I had to get out. I could feel that at any minute I was going to start rushing around wringing my hands and screaming or something.' She choked very slightly on her next words. 'I – I specially didn't want Felicity to see me falling to pieces. Then, when I got back here, I opened up that bottle of Bell's that's been standing unopened in the corner of my cupboard for months, and just swigged some down.' She shuddered. 'Horrible stuff! Doesn't half work quick, though.'

'And the tablets?'

I hadn't wanted to ask, but …

Dip flushed.

'Yes, well, to be honest, my grand attempt at suicide was risibly similar to the times when I've had a bad headache. I had to go rooting around in my two boxes of first-aid stuff, just like I always do, hunting for enough pain-killers to end it all.' Her blush deepened. 'I don't think I was very serious about that side of it. When I said that I'd taken some tablets I was telling the literal truth, because more than one is "some", isn't it? And I'd taken three Dispirin. I'm going to need another two for my head in a minute, except that I haven't got any.'

I felt a great surge of relief.

'I'll get you some.'

It was as I stood up to go and do this that I remembered what had passed through my mind just before driving over to see Dip. Hmm …

'Dip, nothing's actually changed, has it?'

'What do you mean?'

'Well, this morning and everything – it hasn't actually made a difference to what you went through all those years ago. I mean, the feelings of guilt and sadness and the rest of it, they're not going to go away just because you've told me what happened, are they?'

Dip shook her head slowly.

'No,' she said softly, 'the fact that someone else knows does change things a bit, and I'm really glad I told you, and I'd like you to tell Mike as well, if you don't mind, but – no, you're right, it won't make much difference.'

'You see, the other thing you said on the phone was that you'd been drinking damnation to yourself. Do you remember that?'

Dip rubbed her face with the palms of her hands and laughed.

'Oh, Kathy, how very embarrassing! I didn't really

say that, did I? Another spot of over-dramatization there, I'm afraid.'

I waited without speaking. I was capable of doing that sometimes, believe it or not. Dip stopped laughing and went on seriously.

'It is true, though. I've had a sneaking suspicion all my life – well, since, you know, since I was sixteen – that on Sundays God spots me coming up towards the communion rail and shakes his head and says, "Oh, dear, here comes the Reynolds woman, that wicked girl who had the abortion. Look, there she stands, taking up some innocent person's place, eating and drinking damnation to herself. Can't stand the sight of her!" ' She held up a restraining hand. 'Please spare me comforting theology, if that's what you're tempted to come out with. I'm telling you how I feel, not what I believe at the bottom of my heart to be the case. I really think I love God, and I know deep down inside that he loves me – I never have any doubt at all that he loves you Robinsons – but, Kathy, this thing's been an open wound in me for years and years. It feels as if it would hurt just as much in the very heart of heaven, and it just will not even begin to heal.'

I found myself tapping my teeth nervously with a forefinger. The next bit was not going to be easy for me.

'Dip, I'm a bad-tempered, thoughtless person a lot of the time – I know that – and there's no reason that I can think of why God should use an idiot like me for anything at all, but when I was speaking to you on the telephone earlier, I felt sure suddenly, or – or I was sort of *filled up* with knowing for sure, that we ought to have a little communion service, quietly, just in the housegroup, so that God can do something about you and David.' The last drops of confidence drained away as I continued. 'I don't even really know why, or what might happen, but – but I just think maybe we should do it ...'

I hung my head, feeling like one of the gawkish teenage evangelicals I had been and gone around with in the sixties, some of us peddling Ouija-board Christianity for all we were worth to keep the whole thing interesting. Sensing what was going through my mind, Dip smiled reassuringly at me, already starting to settle back into the much more familiar role of unflappable friend and support.

'Kathy, I'll be frank with you, the idea of doing that frightens me rigid, but I do know how difficult it was for you to say that to me, so I think I'd better take notice. Anyway, you can't measure the value of the post by the quality of the postman, can you?'

'You can't – ? Oh, I see what you mean – no, you're right, of course.'

Pause.

'This means the other people in the group will have to know, doesn't it?'

'I suppose it does. I'm not sure. Would you be able ...?'

Dip leaned back in her chair and produced one of those sighs that starts from right down at the bottom of your boots.

'Kathy, I've lived with this for more than forty years, and I think I've been a bit of a coward. I *want* things to change. I'll do whatever it takes.'

'Right. Good. Right. Well, I'll go and get the, err, the tablets.'

'Okay.'

6

Lying cosily in bed that night, I rested my head against my husband's shoulder and held on to one of his arms with both of mine. I actually had every reason to feel sad. Mike had broken the news to me a little earlier that what we had tended to call the 'Australian money' would now have to become the 'new roof' money. I had left it too late, and now the choice had been taken away from me. After what had happened with Dip, though, this seemed relatively trivial, especially as I was able to appreciate the solid warmth of Mike's presence beside me. He was there with his library book, and he was mine. I didn't need to go to the library any more.

I had told Mike all about Dip's problem, and about the rather scary responsibility I had taken for suggesting a communion service that might help her in some way. Mike doesn't cry much, but he had shed a little tear or two for Dip, as I thought he probably would. He sounded quite worried when I mentioned the communion service, though. Now, he laid his book down and turned to me.

'Kathy, you're sure this communion thing is – you know – the right thing to do?'

'I can't talk about being sure, exactly, Mike. I only know that when the idea first came into my mind, it – well, it filled me up with itself. I can't think of another way to put it. It's only happened about twice in my whole life. I know I could be wrong, but I think the most important thing is that I'm more scared of not doing it than doing it.'

He thought for a moment and then nodded.

'All right, but you do know we're quite possibly going to run into some opposition, don't you? Apart from anything else, Simon can't just agree to do something like that without giving it a lot of thought. In fact, I know jolly well he won't. Do you want me to talk to him about it, or will you?'

'Mmm ...'

For a moment or two I pictured myself having the requisite conversation with our housegroup leader. Simon Davenport was a very upright and charitable man, good-looking as well, in a dark, doe-eyed sort of way (Mike said he bore a striking resemblance to Hanse Cronje, the captain of the South African cricket team). Simon did tend, though, to travel along very straight lines in his thinking about Christian topics, greeting most of my contributions to group discussion with a shadow of slight strain on his honest face. He really did conscientiously try to accommodate the views expressed by each member of the group, but there was no doubt that my frequent excursions into the twisting byways and dark alleys of Christian living as actually experienced by human beings were fleas in the vest of desirable progress as far as he was concerned.

'Perhaps, if you mentioned it to him first, Mike, then he'll know it's not just a wild idea. I make him nervous, but he respects you, doesn't he? Then you and I could talk to him and we could meet and pray together, and meanwhile I'll ask God to fix it all for us.'

Mike looked sternly at me.

'Simon would hate to hear you talking like that, as you know full well.'

'I know,' I said drowsily, 'but he's not here, so he can't.'

'You're incorrigible.'

'No, I'm not, I'm Church of England.'

'Do you realize I've been saying you're incorrigible and you've been saying you're not, you're Church of England, ever since we first got married?'

'Well, it's good that there are some things we've gone on doing since we first got married, don't you think?'

'Did you have something particular in mind?'

'Yes, I did, actually. Have you finished your boring old library book yet?'

'Yes, I think I probably have ...'

Sunday

1

'Mum, when's dinner going to be ready?'

'It's ready now, Mark, but we are not having it until Felicity's done her violin practice, so speak to her, not me. I'm sick of telling her. She promised to do it last night but she watched something instead. She said it would be all right because she'd do it before church today and she didn't do it. Then she promised to do it as soon as we got back, but she still didn't do it. She can jolly well do it now or nobody's going to eat today. And you can get the glasses out.'

'Why are you speaking as if you're cross with me?'

'I'm not cross with you, I'm cross with Felicity.'

'Felicity! Come and do your – oh, it's all right, Mum, Dip's helping her.'

'Fine, but as a matter of trivial detail, I haven't heard any violin-playing yet. Call me a slave to habit, but I've rather got into the way of expecting to hear the violin being played when a practice is in progress. Get the glasses out.'

'What's Jack doing, then?'

'I can't hear you over the violin. What did you say?'

'I asked you what Jack's doing?'

'Are you eighteen or four?'

'How many?'

'Six with Dip.'

'Can I have mine on my lap? I'm going out at half past two.'

'You'll have to change your trousers if you're going to have your dinner on your lap. No, you can't.'

'No funnier than last time or the time before that, Mum. Can't we start?'

'Tell everyone to come, and we'll start as soon as Felicity's been through Vivaldi one more time, if Vivaldi can stand it.'

'DINNER, EVERYONE!'

'*I* could have done that, Mark!'

'Why did you ask me to, then?'

Sunday lunchtimes in our house had been many things over the last couple of decades. When the children were small, Mike often talked about how much he was looking forward to future years when these richly traditional occasions would be spiced with good conversation and bright convivial laughter, weekly opportunities for the cementing of good family relationships and the healing of any small rifts that might have occurred during the previous week. A ripple of mildly hysterical inner laughter passes through me when I think of those projections now. As far as I can recall, Mike's charmingly civilized scenario did not allow for such phenomena as two brothers making determined efforts to batter each other's heads in with place-mats in a vicious argument over the last roast potato, nor a wildly irrational wife and mother sending a bowl of steaming hot leeks skating down the length of the table like a curling stone after two of her family had made being-sick noises as soon as the lid was removed – these being two of the more dramatic highlights that sprang immediately to mind. Nor, to my recollection, was there any awareness, in those sweet innocent days before the children excitedly discovered God's wonderful gift of free will, that simply getting all of them to sit down at the table at the same time would so often prove to be a task of considerable magnitude.

For instance, the summer brought televised cricket, a so-called sporting entertainment inducing mystification and fury in me to about the same degree.

The mystification is easily explained. About midway through the morning, all three male Robinsons would hang their brains up in the hall like cycling helmets, disappear to the sitting-room and peer with intense concentration at a screen showing a dozen or so men dressed in white, distributed at random around a large field, doing *absolutely nothing*. Every now and then there would be a burst of applause from the spectators as one of the men did his own little bit of nothing in what one assumes must have been a sparklingly talented way, at which point Mike, Jack and Mark would be galvanized into excited discussion about strategies by which it might have been possible for the individual concerned to have achieved inertia with even greater efficiency.

The fury usually manifested itself at about twelve forty-five, when I would have the effrontery to point out that the dinner I had prepared was ready and on the table, only to be met with groans of frustration because the cricket had reached 'a really crucial stage'.

'But you've been watching it for nearly two hours!' I would scream.

This was the cue for deep, head-shaking sighs of frustrated incredulity at the sheer scope of my idiocy, together with tut-laden groans of disbelief that I was unable to achieve even the most rudimentary grasp of this imbecile game of theirs.

'But that's the whole point!' one of them would sufferingly point out, unbearably burdened by the weight of my denseness. 'The whole morning has been leading up to this last quarter of an hour. A couple of quick dismissals between now and lunch, and by teatime we'll have polished off the tail and passed their total.'

Nonplussed by such volleys of gibberish, I tended to retire tight-lipped to the kitchen and slam things around for a minute or two. Eventually, Mike, vaguely recalling that he was supposed to be a mature adult, would ascend halfway towards the standing position from his chair in the very slowest of slow motion, and, with eyes still fixed on the screen like a rabbit hypnotized by a snake, begin to make painfully gradual progress, still maintaining his strange puppet-like, semi-sitting posture, in the direction of the kitchen. Once he was through the door, vertical again, brain re-inserted, the sight of hot food successfully broke the trance at last, and he would issue peremptory orders to the other two rabbits. He would even, on occasions, with massive unfairness, rebuke them mildly for their selfishness in not coming immediately when their hard-working mother had been to all this trouble to cook them a nice dinner. The amazing thing, on reflection, is that we seemed to go through this little drama once, at the very least, every single summer, as though it had never happened before and none of us knew what our lines or moves were supposed to be.

My only comfort was that this seemed to be the way with many other households. We human families happily (or, at least, resignedly) go through set pieces which must sometimes look quite bizarre to outsiders.

Mike and I witnessed a quite fascinating example of this as we sat on one of the old wrought-iron Victorian seats on our local common one summer afternoon.

A family of four, out for an afternoon stroll, passed us on the satisfyingly elegant tree-lined avenue that runs along the south edge of the common and the cricket-pitch. Dad was in the lead, looking faintly bored and exasperated, yet, at the same time, very responsible and Dad-like. He carried a long, whippy stick in his hand, ready to slash at brambles and beat off any bush monsters that might leap from the undergrowth to attack his wife or his little brood. Half of his little brood followed a few yards behind, a pigtailed girl of about ten, full of oldest-child confidence, leading with her chin and chest, marching along rather than walking. Next came Mum, dressed in precisely the clothes you wear for walking on the common, an exact but larger copy of her daughter, the two of them looking like a couple of those hollow dolls that fit into each other, but with two or three stages left out. The other half of the brood, obviously the youngest in the family, and certainly lowest in the pecking-order as far as this particular little familial farmyard was concerned, was a boy of around six years old, who, at this stage of the walk, had stopped to explore the invitingly accessible lower branches of a horse-chestnut. He was now dangling contentedly by both hands from the lowest branch of the tree, waiting, as small boys so healthily and enviably do, for the next thing to happen.

The next thing to happen was Dad realizing that his small son was lagging behind, and deciding it was time he caught up.

'Leave it!'

Sometimes we parents issue orders to our small children with a military sharpness and acidity that we would never dream of using with anyone else. Fortunately, the extent to which small children respond and give credence to this sort of excess tends to be in directly inverse proportion to the degree of sharpness and acidity injected into the command. Children may be inexperienced, but they're not silly. They seem to be aware at a very early age that, in the mechanics of obedience, frequency invariably outweighs vocal force. That explains why this typical specimen of a small boy continued to dangle happily from his branch despite the parental admonition. He was still a long way from having to do what he was told, and he knew it.

'Leave it!!'

This time Dad slammed the same phrase out like a man hammering a second nail into stubbornly hard wood after bending the first one, and with much greater force than he had used on the first attempt. Innocent folk who never were part of such a family might have assumed quite reasonably at this point that it was bound to do the trick. Such crashing dominance, such threateningly fierce tones, must surely result in the lad instantly dropping to the ground and rushing like the wind to catch up with his father to apologize before some dreadful punishment befell him. Touching naiveté! He continued to dangle, of course.

It was Mum's turn.

'LEAVE IT!'

The sheer venom with which the lad's mother screeched exactly the same pair of words as her mate would have been deeply alarming if Mike and I had not been so aware of the previously mentioned frequency/force equation. Mike whispered that he would have moved like a shot if she'd spoken to him like that, but the little boy we were observing with such interest was possessed of crucial, family-related information. He knew exactly what he was doing. He continued to dangle – and as he dangled, he grinned.

'Leave it!'

This fourth and, as it transpired, final command was transmitted in a lordly squeak by our little hero's sister – she who, at this stage of their lives at any rate, was probably his greatest enemy on the face of the earth. Knowing her power, she had not even bothered to turn her head as she spoke. Gloriously unhampered by the civilized restraints that might have curbed her parents in dealing with their smallest offspring, this girl would be capable, at the correct, expertly judged moment, of doing her brother surgically precise harm when she next encountered him in that unpoliced jungle of a world that is called 'When the grown-ups are not about'.

Four identical directives had been issued, culminating in the boy's worst enemy entering the fray. Clearly, he felt that it was time for the force of gravity to be strategically employed. Dropping lightly to the ground, he scampered to catch the others up – still grinning.

All families are the same, with varying degrees of sophistication. They have their own special, private sets of rules, and their own ways of playing out the same old set-pieces again and again, often in a virtually identical way, not necessarily as a result of being blinkered, but simply because they are *them*.

Ours was no exception. Sunday lunch was traditionally a rather tense occasion in our house, precisely (ludicrously, when one thought about it) because everyone was aware that Mike so wanted it to be relaxed. Five people more or less busting a gut to produce a family idyll that had never really existed in the first place is hardly conducive to relaxation. The best times had always been when Dip was there, not because the children were on their reluctant best behaviour with a visitor – as a matter of history, they weren't – but because she had that hot-water-bottle-y sort of presence that seems to so successfully combat the chilling draughts of ill grace and dispute. Even more important, perhaps, was the very special rapport that existed between her and Mark, whose usual idea of an enjoyable lunch was to get the food down his neck and clear off as soon as we acceded to his mumbled request to be allowed to 'get down'. When Dip was with us he actually seemed to want to be there.

She was with us today, saying less than usual, and a little puffy-eyed if you looked closely, but otherwise just the same.

That Sunday lunchtime, on the day after the Saturday that had been so pervaded by marine odours, was one of our less acrimonious ones – once we had all sat down, that is – but a comparatively detailed recollection of the twists and turns of comment and response during that half hour or so shows just how raggedly complex such occasions could be, and how packed with potential for disaster.

As soon as Felicity had played through her piece for a second time and been sent back to put her violin away, the six of us assembled around our long kitchen table (my favourite piece of furniture, by the way) and Mike began to carve the joint.

'Right!' he said contentedly as he carved. 'How about someone suggesting a really nice family activity for this afternoon, something we can all do together for a change?'

As he spoke the first plate was in the process of being passed to the other end of the table, where Mark distracted anyone who might have been about to answer this question by drawing back in apparent terror at the sight of the generous slices from the joint on his plate.

'This is unlucky meat!' he exclaimed, his voice trembling like one of those gloriously talent-free actors in the early horror movies.

'And why might that be?' enquired Mike calmly, continuing to saw placidly.

'Please,' groaned Jack, 'I don't think we really want to know, do we?'

Felicity wanted to know. She always wanted to know everything.

'Why is it unlucky meat, Mark?'

'Because,' replied Mark in sepulchral tones, 'this is the lamb that gambolled and lost.'

'O-o-oh, good,' said Jack Blackadderishly, apparently greatly relieved. 'I was only worried that it might turn out to be a bad joke, but as it's not a joke at all, that's fine.'

Felicity's frowning gaze was still fixed on Mark.

'Gambled at what?'

'Not gambled – gamb*oll*ed! Gambolled sounds like betted but it means skipped about.'

Felicity looked doubtfully at the plate of meat that had by now appeared in front of her, another more troubled question framing itself on her lips.

'It's not funny when you have to explain it,' complained Mark as he passed the vegetables to his sister.

'Don't worry,' said Jack kindly, 'it's not funny when you don't have to explain it as well.'

'Violin seems to be going very well.'

Dip's bright comment was obviously designed to distract Felicity from the mental image of the collected source of our various dinners skipping happily around a field in its original state.

She nodded and Mike said, 'Yes, she's really come on lately. You're doing quite difficult pieces now, aren't you, darling?'

It was true. Felicity had begun to learn the violin a few years ago, by a Japanese method which demanded the presence of a parent at all lessons. The wretchedly unmusical but available parent in this case had been me. As the weeks went by, I had begun to feel rather like a junior school child myself in my abject fear that Mr Tyson, Felicity's violin teacher, would tell me off if I arrived late for the lesson each Wednesday morning, or if my daughter had demonstrably not practised since the last time. Early in this lengthy learning process the whole family had become accustomed to gritting their teeth and finding ways to survive endless, squeaky repetitions of 'Twinkle, twinkle, little star' in a greater variety of musical forms than it seemed possible for the mind of man or woman to devise.

As time went by, though, Felicity's skill increased dramatically, and now her fingers fairly flew up and down the neck of her three-quarter-size instrument.

The trickiest aspect of it all, no-one will be surprised to hear, was getting her to practise. My arsenal in this ongoing warfare consisted of encouragement, threats, bribes, the occasional parental sulk, fury, flattery, shouting very loudly, coaxing very gently, making her cry, making her laugh and presenting her with cosmically awful, end-of-the-world-as-we-know-it alternatives. Jack's idea was the one that worked longest and best. He suggested putting a small sweet or trinket under an upturned cup in the practice area and letting Felicity have it when the session was finished. This device, one of the many ploys I would have scorned in those dear sweet days when children were purely hypothetical, really appealed to her, and got us through the most difficult patch of all. Nowadays she still had to be pressured into practising, but her music really did seem to have become part of who she was. She could actually *play* the violin, and even enjoy it. My daughter could play the *violin*! I was amazed every time I thought about it.

'Felicity, could I ask you a question about your violin music? There's something that's been puzzling me.'

Felicity looked suspiciously at her older brother as he poured gravy over the pile of food on his plate. Jack's jokes always started very seriously.

'What about it?'

'You see, I had the idea that usually at the top of a sheet of music, it says something like "Sprightly, with an air of freedom", or "Loudly, and with passion", something like that. Don't they usually say something of that sort?'

'Might do. Dunno. Why?'

'Well, your music is quite different from that, isn't it? I noticed at the top of one of them it says, "Reluctantly, and with an air of resentment", and on the other one it says, "Morosely, and with little grunting sounds of annoyance". Perhaps that's why you've found practising so difficult. You're following the instructions too closely.'

Felicity speared a piece of hot roast potato, popped it in her mouth and spoke through and round it with exaggerated, compensatory clarity.

'You and Mark should go and tell your sad jokes about skipping sheep and things at the top of music to some people who are fed up with laughing and want to have a serious time for a while.'

'Don't eat with your mouth full, Felicity,' I corrected automatically. 'What are you all laughing about? Oh – you knew what I meant.'

'Speaking of people who are fed up with laughing,' said Mike, when everyone had subsided, 'reminds me – Kathy, did you hear what Norman Davis said to me in church today?'

'No,' I replied, recalling mainly my relief that there had been no sign of Joscelyn and John in their normal places near the front that morning. 'I saw him lean over towards you, but I couldn't hear what he was saying. Now you mention it, it did strike me that he was looking almost happy. I thought there must be something wrong with him.'

We had known this Norman Davis fellow for years through the church community, and in all that time he had been about as far removed from being a twinkling little sunbeam of a person as you could imagine. On the contrary, he was what you might call a stubbed-toe of a man, hot, angry and full of some kind of throbbing misery. Norman sat through most of our services like a man being tried for murder who has just caught sight of the black cap on the judge's desk. That morning Mike and I had nodded amiably at him as we took our seats in the same row for the communion service, and we had smiled at each other when he responded with his usual negative shrug and a dark grimace hinting at untold depths of unhappiness caused by *them*, the ones who, in Norman's world, were always out to get us all. I had to confess that I was rather fond of Norman, who, like Eeyore, was a very kind and generous person despite his pessimistic outlook.

'It was just before the congregation started to go up to the altar rail for communion,' said Mike, laying down his knife and fork to tell the story. 'I just happened to glance to my right and I could feel myself doing one of those perfect double-takes they do in comedy films. And the reason was that Grumpy Norman looked transfigured. His eyes shone. There was a big broad smile on his face – I don't think those smiling muscles have had much exercise for a long time – and he was sitting up straight in his chair, more sort of buoyant than I've ever seen him in church before. Dear old Norman, he looked to me as if he might be on the verge of doing an ascension all of his own out of the chair and through the ceiling. I really thought to myself, "This man's been touched by God!" I wondered what amazing revelation had been vouchsafed to the brother on my right to account for such an unusual infilling of joy. And I think he must have noticed out of the corner of his eye that I was watching him, because just then he leaned towards me, this extraordinary light still burning in his eyes, and – well, what do you think he said?'

We all chewed in Mike's direction like a herd of super-domesticated cows and shook our heads interestedly.

'He nodded towards the vicar, and whispered ecstatically, "He's forgotten to do the Peace!"'

Felicity looked puzzled and Mark shuddered darkly, but the rest of us fell about. The 'Exchanging of the Peace', for those who are not familiar with Anglican peculiarities, was the latest attempt (that meant it had only been around for a few decades) by the good old C of E to bring a little informality into some of our services. The idea was that people would move around the church, shaking hands or hugging each other and verbally offering the Peace of the Lord to one another. Some folk, and Norman had always been one of them, dreaded and disliked this practice intensely. After years of shoving up KEEP OUT! signs at the edge of your personal space even in informal situations, I suppose it must be a kind of torture to be expected to do it artificially. Mike had been wrong in his initial diagnosis of Norman's transfiguration. There had been no spiritual revelation, just gleeful relief.

'I hated that too, when I used to go,' said Mark through a mouthful of food, sounding as if he was talking about an experience of putting his foot in something unpleasant by accident. 'People I didn't know used to come up to me and act like I was their best friend suddenly. One woman kissed me once. Ugh! Glad I don't have to go now. I hate church *so* much.'

2

Silence fell around the table as everyone bent busily to their plates. It was as though an invisible person had issued a general order that no-one was to speak for a limited period. Actually, it was to do with what had just been said, and what I might be about to say. Out of the corner of my eye I saw Mike glance at me. He knew exactly what my reaction to Mark's comment was likely to be.

Some years earlier, when Mark was fourteen, he had pleaded, initially through the mediation of Dip, who was obviously far less likely to bite his head off than me, to be allowed to stop going to church because he hated and loathed it and the weekly inevitability of attending was 'spoiling the rest of his life', according to him. Mike and I had agreed, as long as he still came along on what we regarded as special times, a condition which he agreed to, but actually complied with only after considerable pressure on each occasion. This Easter, for instance, full of chocolate and ill grace, he had morosely endured the Sunday service, declaring afterwards that he would be 'well pleased' if he never had to step through the doors of a church ever again.

The agreement that Mark need not come to church any more was made with considerable reluctance on my part. It made me feel such a failure as a parent and as a Christian. Mark's tendency at that time to just disappear in the evenings and at weekends with a shadowy group of friends, characterized by their hooded eyes and mechanically strategic expressions of politeness, meant that I spent frequent sleepless nights wondering what kinds of dark villainy might be going on out there in the wild teenage world. Like many a parent before me, I had dreamed *The Waltons,* but feared I had woken up to *Trainspotting.* Telling Mark he no longer had to go to church felt like deliberately throwing him into the middle of the night. As it turned out, he seemed, by and large, to have survived whatever dark and terrible things he might have been engaged in, and he was now at the local college of further education, battling through an A level course in Communication Studies and History which seemed, to my weary perception, to have been going on for about fifteen years so far. Nowadays he spent most of his free time with two fairly mild, skinny friends with tadpole-like large heads, who were on the same college course. Jason and Richard, whose eyes were certainly not hooded, succeeded in gulping out rudimentary pleasantries at appropriate times, but generally suffered a purple paralysis of embarrassment in the presence of Mike or me.

All in all, things were certainly better with my second oldest son than I would have dared to hope a few years ago, but the business of church still hurt and troubled me on quite a deep level. It seemed to me infuriatingly insensitive of Mark to be so mindlessly, thoughtlessly scathing about such an important part of our lives, and in front of everyone else. Irrationally, it struck me as even worse that he should have done it at Sunday lunch, but then my dealings with Mark were not famous for the flow of reason which swept them to their frequently half-drowned conclusions. At Mark's words, the all too familiar wave of anger had begun to rise in me, together with the knowledge that I would either have to pursue what he had said to its bitter, lunch-disrupting end, or stuff it all back inside again, grit my teeth, and smash a cup or something later when I was on my own. Selecting the teeth-gritting option, I was still unable to restrain myself from stabbing my fork with unnecessary force against my china dinner-plate. My dear daughter noticed, of course.

'What's the matter, Mummy?'

'Just releasing a little tension, darling – nothing much. Eat up.'

'Why do people say eat up, instead of eat down? The food goes down, doesn't it, not up, except when you're … Was it what Mark said?'

Dip tapped the table with her forefinger to attract Felicity's attention.

'Hey, can you think of an answer to your dad's question, Felicity? No-one else has.'

'Sorry, Mum,' mumbled Mark, rightly interpreting a meaningful look from his father.

If you know you've upset your mum with something you've said, for goodness' sake just say sorry, and that'll probably be the end of it.

I could almost hear Mike's voice advising his son at some quiet moment on how to deal with the resident loony when things got explosive. If I gritted my teeth much more they would begin to crumble under the pressure. I leaned an elbow on the table and rested my forehead in my hand. I didn't want to pick up Mark's used tissue of an apology on this occasion. Why should I? In my head I formed the words and sentences that would erupt from me if I decided to forget about restraint. It would be so easy and so releasing to let it all out. Why *should* I have to put up with people saying hurtful things and colluding over the best way to prevent me from reacting in whichever way I wanted? It made me so *mad* …! I sent out imaginary bubbles containing imaginary swearwords that burst over Mark's head and showered him with my anger.

'It was about doing something together,' said Mike, firmly jolly. 'You'd like us to have a family outing this afternoon, wouldn't you, Kathy?'

'Can we go bowling and have a pizza?' asked Felicity.

'If you pay, Flitty,' teased Jack, flipping his hand across the top of her head, pretending to hit her.

'*Wouldn't* you, Kathy?'

Blow you, Mike!

'Yes,' I mumbled, 'I s'pose it would be nice to go out somewhere.'

'Can I ring a friend and ask her to come, and can she stay the night afterwards?'

'No!' chorused the rest of the family, united at least in this, their reluctance to spend an afternoon in the high-pitched, lisping presence of Caroline Burton.

'I didn't mean Caroline,' lied Felicity shamelessly, 'I meant Jenny.'

'No, darling,' said Mike firmly, 'we want to go out as a family for once. You see plenty of Jenny and Caroline without them coming today. Let's just be us for a change.'

Mark glared significantly at his father.

'Dad!'

Mike stared blankly back at his son, presumably puzzled by such unprecedented and vehement support of Felicity's right to invite a friend.

'I just meant that it would be nice for once to –'

Dip interrupted, laying a hand on Mike's arm and smiling imperturbably as she spoke.

'I think Mark was very kindly pointing out that I'm not actually a member of the family, Mike, but the very fact that you said what you said in front of me shows that you do think of me as being a sort

99

of part of you all, so I really wouldn't worry about it.'

I look forward with interest to the day that must eventually come, when my husband will blush with such intensity and heat that he spontaneously combusts. His babblingly incoherent apologies to Dip just made us all laugh, while Felicity jumped from her chair and made a special trip round the table to lean affectionately against someone whom she certainly regarded, quite unequivocally, as an extra member of the family.

'I know exactly what we ought to do this afternoon.'

There was a hush, partly caused by surprise. It was a rather unusual thing for Mark to make such a definite statement about anything to do with the family as a whole. I think we all felt mildly excited, as though an unexpectedly special occasion had arisen.

'I thought you were going out at half-past two. That's why you wanted your dinner on your lap, according to you earlier.'

'Oh, I was, but I can phone. I'd rather do this if everyone wants to.'

'Go on, then.'

'Right! You know that big glass jar in the kitchen that we put pennies and tuppences in?'

'Ye-e-es,' said Mike suspiciously, visibly preparing himself to say no to something that would involve wasting money. 'What about it?'

The degree of animation in Mark was quite riveting in its unexpectedness.

'Well, here's what we ought to do, right? We go down to the sea and we park in one of those slanting sort of places under the grassy hill near the big hotel, right? And Felicity brings her roller-blades and Jack and I bring a tennis ball or a cricket ball, right? And we walk along towards the pier with Mum and Dip talking, and Dad sometimes catching the ball with Jack and me and sometimes talking to Mum and Dip, and Felicity roller-blading along and moaning about not having a friend with her, right?'

Mark stopped for breath.

We all said, 'Right?'

'Then, when we get to the pier, that's when we do the first really good thing, right?'

Mike was looking increasingly uneasy, but Felicity had moved slowly nearer and nearer to her brother as he spoke, until now she was standing right by his shoulder, totally concentrated on his face and on the scenario that he was developing.

'What's the first really good thing, Mark?' she asked eagerly.

'Hot doughnuts!' exclaimed Mark triumphantly. 'Just by the entrance to the pier there's a place that sells doughnuts, fresh-cooked, all hot and covered in sugar. If you get ten you only have to pay for eight. Really nice! Just think about it for a moment, and I know for a fact they're open on Sundays.'

'Well, I'm beginning to like the sound of this, even if no-one else is,' said Dip with enthusiasm.

'So,' said Mike hopefully, 'that's where the, err, the coins from the jar come in, we use just a few of them for the doughnuts, right?'

'*Oh*, no! The coins are for the second really good thing.'

Mark glanced around the table to check that his audience was paying proper attention. He must have been gratified. Everyone was aching to know what the second really good thing might be.

'After we've had our doughnuts,' he continued, 'we take the jar with all the coins into the amusement arcade on the pier and we all have lots and lots of goes on the thing where you put a coin in the slot and it pushes other coins over the edge in a sort of waterfall into the cup underneath, and those are the ones you win.'

Felicity clapped her hands delightedly at this idea, but I observed that the blood supply was draining away from poor Mike's face as quickly as it had suffused it a few moments ago.

'Now *that*,' commented Jack warmly, 'is what I call a very good idea. I remember when I was a kid I always wanted to have enough money to be able to have a go on one of those and have a lot of fun and not worry about using money that was supposed to be for something else. Let's do it, Dad!'

'The amusement arcade?' Mike managed to make the proposition sound as doomladen as if Mark had suggested a short excursion into the depths of Hades just to have a scout round for the afternoon to see if we might prefer it to heaven. 'I really don't think that's on, do you, Kath? Not really ...'

Looking at Mark's expression of proud initiation and the enthusiasm on the faces of Jack and

Felicity, I decided that this was not an appropriate moment to offer automatic support to my husband.

'Why not, Mike?'

Pause.

'Why not? Why *not*? Well, surely that doesn't need spelling out, does it?'

Everyone nodded unhelpfully.

'Well,' began Mike, looking round at his audience of non-spellers, 'I mean, apart from anything else, it's not the sort of place that – I don't know – well, for a start, there'll probably be lots of kids from the school hanging around, and it feels sort of …'

'There'll be hardly anyone else there around four o'clock, Dad,' offered Mark reassuringly. 'I've been down there at that time on a Sunday loads of times. It's nearly empty usually.'

Mike still looked very doubtful indeed.

'Mmm, but we did say we were going to save that change for a rainy day. It seems an awful waste to just blow it on this machine thing you're talking about.'

Jack glanced towards the window.

'Quite a bit of cloud about, Dad. I reckon it'll qualify as a rainy day by the time we get down there. Come on, let's just *do* it. Sometimes it's good to do things you never do.'

Mike once more surveyed the ring of eager faces around the table, clearly teetering on the edge of reluctant agreement. But it was too much for him.

'No,' he said, shaking his head and looking strangely similar to the father at the head of the

'Leave it' procession, 'I can tell you three very good reasons why this is a bad idea.'

He ticked them off on his fingers as he addressed the staff group.

'First, it really is a terrible waste of the money that we've been putting into that jar for the last couple of months. Second, whatever Jack says, you can't really be a hundred per cent sure who'll be at a place like that and I do have my dignity to consider. Third, and most important in my view, betting on slot machines is not a good example for Christians to offer the rest of the world. There's something seedy and unpleasant about the idea that you set out to win money you haven't earned by gambling – not that I would expect us to win any money anyway. I'm quite sure those machines are fixed. Lastly, I know I wouldn't enjoy it at all and I'd be worried that I'd probably make everyone else feel miserable as well.'

'That's four things,' commented Mark morosely.

'The walk along the front and perhaps the – the, err, doughnuts would be very nice,' continued Mike, 'but –' he shook his head again ' – I think the arcade is out, I'm afraid.'

Felicity went sulkily back to her place. We sat in silence for a moment. I served pudding. Sadly for the plans Mike and I were formulating to inject a little extra romance into our marriage, my over-whelming inclination at this juncture was to empty the trifle bowl over my husband's head. I seriously contemplated doing exactly that for a moment – not violently, you understand, but with a calm, definite, downward movement that would extinguish his so-called dignity with squishy, sticky completeness. The briefest reflection suggested that, although this would be extremely satisfying for me, it was unlikely to bring us any nearer to our desired objective. Mark caught my eye and grimaced. I grimaced back in sympathy. Rare, to say the least. That was what decided me. We were going to take those coins and we were all going to use them in that machine on the pier.

'Mike?'

'Yes, Kathy? Beautiful trifle, by the way.'

He sounded nervous.

'Thank you, Mike.' I continued in what Jack calls my 'padded steel' voice. 'Mike, I think that Mark's idea is an excellent one in every respect, and I would like to say that the reasons you've put forward for not doing what he suggests are not just weak, but almost totally without form or substance.'

'We *are* going,' I heard Felicity whisper happily under her breath to Jack.

I leaned back in my chair, and laid both hands flat on the table.

'Let us take those reasons of yours in reverse order, shall we? Number one – you wouldn't enjoy it, and therefore you're deeply concerned that you might make the rest of us miserable. Have I got that right?'

'Err, yes, that's right, yes …'

'Okay, let's have a little vote, shall we? Hands up all those who will become so miserable because Daddy is standing just outside the amusement arcade *not* enjoying it, while we're inside enjoying it, that we won't want to do it? Come on, hands up, please! As I thought. Totally unanimous. No need to worry on that score, Mike. Second point –' I waved a hand in his direction '– no, please, no need to comment. Second point, it's a bad example for people who aren't Christians, right?'

'Yes, it's a –'

'Well, each of us has to make an individual decision about these things, according to our conscience, don't we?'

'Yes, but –'

'And as Christians we are free, are we not?'

'Yes, but only as long as –'

'So, we'll all use our freedom to go and play on the machines, while you stand outside and use yours to tell everybody that it's not a very good idea to go in.'

'That's one of the most ridiculous –'

'The third reason was something to do with your little charges seeing their noble headmaster doing something as crass and undignified as enjoying himself with his family. Well, how about if the rest of us all pretend to be a bit peculiar, and you tell any of your pupils who come along that we're a hostel outing you've volunteered to take charge of during the weekend, and that they must be very kind and nice to us, because we're just the same as everyone else really?'

'We could pretend that we're all looking after Mark,' suggested Jack. 'I think most people would find that perfectly feasible.'

'We could put a collar and lead on Mark,' added Felicity, 'and make him catch bits of doughnut in his mouth so people put money in a hat like busters. You'd like that, wouldn't you, Marky-boy?'

'I'll catch *you* in a minute,' said Mark, 'and when I do I'm going to tickle you until you scream. Anyway, it's buskers. Are we going, Dad?'

'Hold on,' I interrupted, 'I haven't come to the last point yet, the one about it being a waste of money. Just how much money do you think there is in that jar, Mike? Do you think there might be five pounds, or seven pounds, or even perhaps ten pounds? What do you reckon?'

Mike rolled his eyes helplessly and shrugged.

'I don't know – maybe seven or eight pounds, something like that, I should think.'

'Okay, let's say there's eight pounds, right? We're talking about a family outing –'

'Including Dip,' interposed Felicity with primly conscious virtue.

'You're talking about a family outing, including Dip – thank you very much, Twitty-Poos – for six people on a Sunday afternoon, that's going to cost no more than eight pounds for absolutely everything. Now, if that isn't good value and an excellent use of money, I'm a Dutch cobbler's toast-rack.'

'Gallon of petrol?'

Mike's feeble attempt to sound as if he was putting forward the one explosively crucial factor capable of dynamiting my entire counter-argument was pathetic, and he knew it. We were looking at a defeated man.

'So, can someone *please* tell us whether we're going or not?' implored Mark, hanging his head in mock exhaustion.

'What's a Dutch cobbler's toast-rack?'

'Dip,' Mike appealed to her as if she was the only other rational adult in the room, 'you agree with me, don't you? Tell us what you think we should do.'

'It's not my place to tell you what to do,' replied Dip seriously. 'I unequivocally refuse to comment on Mark's excellent suggestions, and if I happened to believe that it would do all of us in general and you more than most an awful lot of good to do something really silly for once, I would certainly not even consider putting forward such a point of view. You are the head of this family and you must make the final decision. Who's coming with me in my car?'

'Me!' Felicity shot her hand up as if she was in class.

'Very well, if you all feel as strongly as that, I suppose we'll go.' Mike spoke with conscious heroism, as one might speak who feels he has battled long and hard on the side of right and been forced to go down with colours flying. 'But let me publicly register the fact that I don't agree with wasting money on this machine thing, and let me also make it quite plain that I shall not be participating myself. Is that clear?'

We all nodded solemnly in response to this pompous little speech, except for Mark, who seemed to be miles away.

'Mark, are you listening? Is that clear?'

'What? Oh, yeah, sorry, Dad, I was just working out what we'll each get when we divide eight pounds by five instead of six.'

'What's a Dutch cobbler's toast-rack?' asked Felicity once more.

'It was just Mumsy trying to be clever,' explained Jack, 'it doesn't mean anything.'

She pondered briefly. 'What's clever about saying something that doesn't mean anything?'

'Nothing, Felicity,' I said, forestalling Jack, 'absolutely nothing at all. Finish your pudding, then we can clear the table and go out.'

3

Jack's semi-humorous prediction about the weather proved to be absolutely accurate. By the time Mike, Jack and I pulled into one of the many available diagonal parking spaces on the other side of the road from the white-painted facade of the Grand Hotel half an hour later, it really had become the rainy day that those coins had been set aside for. Far from putting us off, this kind of weather was a real bonus. Robinsons are rain freaks, and even Dip had been persuaded to join us on one lunatic but memorable occasion when we had all gone mad on the apparatus at the children's recreation ground in the middle of a cloud-burst. This afternoon it was no more than a steady drizzle that was falling, but we were well equipped with three vast golfing umbrellas bought at a car boot sale a few weeks previously. As we locked the car and looked around for the other three I could almost taste the jam in the doughnut that, as Jack had put it in the car, had my name on it.

'There they are,' said Jack, pointing, 'the giant mushroom on top of the slope.'

Silhouetted against the slate-grey expanse of the southern sky, on the very crest of the hill, Dip, Mark and Felicity were gazing towards the distant horizon as they huddled beneath the hugest of our huge umbrellas. They did indeed look like a vast mushroom with a wide, misshapen stalk. As we watched, a small, irregularly shaped piece of the stalk detached itself, turned and began to wave wildly in our direction. Felicity had spotted us.

'Come on!'

Scorning the umbrella I offered him, Jack set off up the grassy slope at a brisk pace towards Felicity, who, with arms held wide and scarf flapping, came pirouetting down the hill like a sycamore seed-pod in the wind to meet her brother.

'Come on, Mike, let's catch him up – show him we're not in our dotage yet.'

'I suppose I might be permitted time to attend to the zip on my coat.'

I have never really understood why Mike ever bothers to sulk. The children, and anyone else who knows him well and happens to be around, always tease him unmercifully until he returns to normal. But then he never was what I would call a *real* sulker, certainly not an expert like me. In fact, he was as moderate in this area as he was in everything else that he did. He indulged in about one sulk a year, rather like my great-uncle Robert with his famous packet of cigars that lasted for a decade, but whenever he did decide to publicly advertise a grievance, his technique was certainly worth studying. One invariable aspect of this was that he started to sound a bit like Bertie Wooster's manservant, Jeeves, on those memorable occasions when the young master has refused to let him dispose of a violet cummerbund or a pair of yellow socks.

'Yes,' I replied in a similarly pompous tone, 'I think it might be possible to permit you that amount of time, and then perhaps we might both be permitted to join the rest of the company at the summit of this incline.'

'Why are you talking in that funny way?'

'Because *you* are.'

'I am not, I just said I needed time to do my coat up. That's perfectly reasonable, wouldn't you say? Anyway, what are they doing up there? I was under the impression that Mark's famous agenda commenced with a walk along the promenade, not an exhausting climb in the opposite direction against the wind to the coldest point on the seafront. I'm not going up there. I'll meet you down by the bathing huts in a minute.'

He began to trudge miserably away around the base of the hill, but stopped and turned after a few yards, as if something had occurred to him.

'Err, Kathy, who's got that money, by the way?'

Annoying as Mike was being, I couldn't help

feeling a little sorry for him at this point. When you've got a good sulk on the brew it's always galling to have to engage in conversation of a practical nature. You know the sort of thing I mean. How do you maintain the arctic bleakness in the eyes and the voice dulled by cruel bruises to the spirit when you're only asking for the potatoes to be passed? It's jolly hard work. You have to put everything you've got into sounding as if a major battle has been fought and won against all the odds. Sympathetic though I may have felt, however, I wasn't going to let him get away with it.

'Pardon? I didn't catch that.'

Even worse than having to ask your practical question is being forced to repeat it. Mike sighed deeply, shudderingly, from the diaphragm, apparently goaded beyond endurance.

'I simply enquired as to who actually has the money.'

'What money's that, then?'

'The coins – you know, the money we saved in the jar on the side. The money that this afternoon is all – Kathy, don't be obtuse, you know perfectly well what I'm talking about. Who has actually brought the money?'

'Me. Obtuse little me. I've got it.'

I patted my leather shoulder-bag enticingly. On hearing the heavy, pleasantly horsey jingling sound, Mike took a step forward and extended a hand.

'Perhaps it would be better if I –'

'Oh, I think not,' I trilled, with ghastly play-group-style brightness, 'because, you see, darling, if I let you take this money, we all know what's likely to happen, don't we? I think we might be sharing two doughnuts between all of us, and having one go each on the machine, mightn't we, and that wouldn't be much fun at all, would it, sweetheart? So –' I reached into the bag and let a couple of handfuls of coins run through my fingers as audibly as possible. 'I'll just hang on to this until it's all been spent, shall I?'

Mike fumed silently. Not only had he failed to wrest control of the cash from me, but he had also lost sulking ground without gaining anything in exchange. Presumably in the hope of salvaging an inch or two of lost progress, he moved back into bleak and dulled mode.

'I'll see you down by the bathing huts,' he mumbled, turning his collar up and trudging away with little faltering steps, for all the world like some convalescent invalid out for his first tentative walk after a lengthy illness.

Meeting Mark at the crest of the hill after I had struggled breathlessly to the top to join the others was an unusually warming experience. More often than I cared to admit, the unwieldy burden of under-acknowledged and unfinished business between us meant that he and I found it difficult even to allow our eyes to meet. It was so good to be able to smile collusively at him as I indicated Mike's distant figure below us, dolefully wending its way towards the seafront.

'Dad's still sulking,' I explained, and I patted my shoulder-bag. 'He tried to get his hands on the money, but I put him straight.'

'Well done, Mum,' said Mark, slapping me vigorously on the back. 'Next stop the pier. Dad'll soon cheer up when he's got a couple of doughnuts inside him. Come on, Flit, let's catch Dad up and see if we can get him really mad by making him laugh. Beat you to the bottom of the hill!'

They raced away, followed at a more modest pace by Dip and me, sharing an umbrella, and Jack strolling a few yards behind us. There were tears in my eyes. I sometimes think that God must install a kind of automatically refuelled, hope-renewing unit in us when we first become parents. A pathetically small but positive interaction with my younger son had succeeded in flooding a dark place inside me with light, and, crazily, it was as though the darkness had never been there in the first place. Now, on this day, in this place, it was all right, and therefore, for all I knew, it might be all right for ever.

I half turned my head towards Dip, intending to tell her how I was feeling, but checked myself quickly. Normally I shared everything with my friend without even thinking about it, but now, remembering my crassness yesterday, and bearing in mind the things she had told me, I suddenly felt very unsure. Perhaps all the rules had changed. I studied the grass around my feet as we walked, and kept quiet.

We had gone only a few more steps when Dip, looking steadily out in the direction of the ocean as she spoke, said very seriously, 'Kathy, do you want to go on being my friend?'

I looked at her, filled with confusion and alarm. What could she possibly mean? How could there be the slightest shadow of a doubt in Dip's mind that I wanted to go on being her friend? I was conscious of my jaw muscles making my mouth open and shut like a dummy, as if somebody else was operating the mechanism. I couldn't make any words come out, however hard I tried.

'Do you want to go on being my friend, Kathy? Tell me you do.'

I shook my head in puzzlement. It was like those times when you nip out to make the tea during a television programme. Somewhere along the line I must have missed one whole chunk of dialogue. Or perhaps I was just too stupid to understand what she was talking about. It happened to me sometimes. My mind seemed so busy flying forwards that I missed things anyone else would have noticed along the way. Maybe that was dignifying it too much. Maybe I was just far more naive than I cared to admit.

A memory from childhood surfaced at that precise moment. I was almost physically rocked with the clarity of its images and the undiluted pungency of associated emotions that must have been tucked carefully away inside my brain for more than forty years.

I was seven, and it was the day before the junior school sports. Miss Crane, our skinny, bad-tempered teacher, had marched us up in a neat crocodile to the nearby cricket ground to practise the sack race and the three-legged race and all the other contests in which we were due to compete on the following day when our mummies and daddies would be there. I really was looking forward to the sports. For some reason I had a fixed notion that I would definitely be very talented at the sack race. I'd rehearsed it in my head over and over again every night as I lay in bed, until I was perfect. Perhaps even more important, I had a three-legged partner all lined up to shoot her hand in the air when we were asked who was going to be racing with who. That was good enough for me. The only fly in the ointment was Miss Crane. You never quite knew what Miss Crane was going to do or say. She was very strict. Once, in the classroom, she had sat down at the piano and started us off singing one of our favourite songs, then stopped us when we were halfway through the first verse, and made us write out the words of three whole songs because some of the girls in the desks at the back had sung the wrong, silly words to one of the tunes in music last week.

On arriving at the cricket ground Miss Crane had made us sit in a tidy row at the edge of the pitch so that she could tell us what to do. It was lovely being there instead of in the classroom. The sun was smiling, the sky was as blue as a hedge-sparrow's egg that my daddy had showed me earlier that year, and the shining green grass felt dry and soft to the touch. And it was sports day tomorrow! Sitting there in the bottle-green tops and little white shorts that we all wore for PT, I bent forward over my knees and rubbed the front of my legs excitedly with the palms of my hands.

'Right!' said Miss Crane crossly. 'Before we start, I don't want anyone trying to tell me how to do my job. Anybody *not* understand that?'

I didn't, but I wasn't going to let Miss Crane know that. Tell her how to do her job? Miss Crane, who went off like a volcano when someone spoke in quiet-reading time, and kept a piece of bamboo for caning naughty people's hands – tell her how to do her job? In any case, how would any of us have been able to tell her how to do her job? She was the teacher. We were the children. We didn't know how to be a teacher. Maybe, I thought, it was something to do with the lavatory. Her job. Big jobs – little jobs. For a while now I had been nursing an uneasy feeling that everything I didn't understand was probably connected in some way with going to the lavatory. I stared at Miss Crane in horror. Surely not! Could she, for some reason beyond my under-standing, be saying that we mustn't tell her how to go to the lavatory? Was one of us likely to do that? A little silent scream rose and fell in me at the thought. It spoiled the sports for me, and then I forgot about it for forty-three years.

It felt a bit like that now with Dip – the same sort of panic because I didn't understand what was being said to me, and the same fear that there might be some underlying factor I wasn't going to like. Dip was talking – almost pleading, as if I'd just said something really alienating or unpleasant. Why should she be entreating me to go on being her friend when nothing I'd said or done could have remotely suggested that I would ever want to be anything else? I found my voice at last.

'Dip, you know – you *know* I want to be your friend. Why – ?'

'In that case, please do say what you were about to say just now, but didn't.'

The rain had stopped, making umbrellas more trouble than they were worth in the gusty wind. I lowered the big, brightly coloured one I had been holding over both of us, rolled it inexpertly and fastened the Velcro bits together.

'You know, Dip, my father would have been horrified to hear that our family has to buy new umbrellas more or less every twelve months. I'm pretty sure he had the same neat black brolly for thirty years, and it never wore out because he mostly only used it on days when it wasn't actually raining but there was a chance in a hundred that it might. I don't suppose the silly thing ever managed to get wet, come to think of it.' I tried to chortle merrily, and failing, swallowed hard. 'Err, I was about to say how marvellous it was to be slapped on the back by Mark and have him say "well done", instead of both of us glaring, or not even looking at each other properly.'

'And you stopped because …?'

'Well, I'm not quite sure – after yesterday, you know, how much to say about the – the children. I don't want you to feel –'

'Kathy,' said Dip firmly, turning her head and looking at me at last, 'if I thought that the things I said yesterday were going to prevent you from talking openly to me about anything under God's sun, and especially your children, I would be more disappointed in our friendship than I can say.'

'Even if I'm – I'm moaning about them?'

'*Especially* if you're moaning about them. I want to be part of it, really part of it and them. I'm sorry I used that word yesterday, but it honestly isn't how I usually feel.' Her eyes shone with laughter suddenly. 'I have some of my most beautiful thoughts when you're complaining about your children.'

I pondered this. A compliment? Possibly, possibly not. It didn't really matter, because my friend was still my friend and she wanted to hear about my children – even if I moaned. I hadn't realized until just now what a gap would have been created in my life by the feeling that I had to watch my tongue when speaking to Dip.

Thank you.

'They've caught Dad up,' said Jack, drawing level with us. He watched for a moment then laughed out loud. 'Look, Dad's trying to chuck a tennis ball around without coming out of his sulk. Not easy. We'll have some fun when it comes to the doughnuts, won't we?'

4

By the time we reached the pier, having satisfactorily completed the ball-throwing, the Mum-and-Dip-talking and the Felicity-roller-blading-and-moaning-about-not-having-a-friend items on our agenda, our little party was together again, and Mark and Felicity were clamouring like three-year-olds for change from my magic bag with which to buy doughnuts.

Situated just inside the entrance to the pier, the hot doughnut emporium was a bright, crudely painted booth conceived and built for sunnier times. It was staffed on this wind-lashed day by one of those intensely miserable girls of about sixteen or seventeen who look as if they are the only one of their friends and contemporaries to have missed the last bus to happiness. This one had sixties-style hair waving down to her shoulders, making her face look the shape of a melted egg-timer, and a mouth heavily made up with dark lipstick. In its pouting unhappiness, it reminded me for some reason of the neck of an old plimsoll bag I'd had as a child, after you pulled the string tight.

One could hardly blame this girl for looking miserable, I thought. Finding yourself stranded beside a pile of unsold doughnuts at the end of a windswept pier on a grey and rainy day in a town that was virtually deserted must have fallen a long way short of her most cherished hopes and dreams. The arrival of six whole customers didn't seem to brighten her up much either, especially when Mark insisted that our ten doughnuts had to be hot ones, as advertised, and not taken from the sad little pile that we assumed she had prepared earlier to cope with an apocryphal rush. The poor girl's clear conviction that she was in some kind of outer waiting-room of hell must have been confirmed

when Mark and Felicity poured a stream of one-
and two-pence pieces on to the counter in front of
her, and began to count out the amount she had
asked for.

'There you are,' said Mark cheerfully, when they
had completed their task, 'it's all there, but I expect
you'll want to check it, won't you?'

We drew aside from the booth, leaving its
proprietor to count coins in a pursed and acid
silence. Unabashed, Mark held the two bags of
doughnuts out towards us, one in each hand.

'Right, there are ten doughnuts and six of us,
which is ten divided by six, which comes to-o-o-o
one and four-sixths, which is the same as, err …'

This would normally have been my husband's
cue to interrupt with the solution to the sum. He
always interrupted people when they were trying
to work things out in their heads. Not this time,
though. Standing a little apart from the rest of us,
hunched against the cold like Captain Oates
wishing he'd not been quite so generous, Mike
bounced very slightly on his heels with frustration
and just about managed to avoid breaking out of
his sulk to tell us all that we could have one and
two-thirds of a doughnut each.

'One and two-thirds,' announced Mark at last.
'I'll break 'em up.'

'No! I'll break them up,' shrilled Felicity, 'I know
you. My third'll end up just a squashy bit.'

'Are you saying you don't trust me?'

'Yes,' said Felicity with feeling, quite unmoved
by Mark's air of deep hurt and indignation, 'you

did it with the chocolate bread the other day. Let Jack do it. Jack, you do mine.'

'Oh, you trust him, then?'

'Of course she does,' said Jack. 'Quite right, too. When I was at school they used to call me Abacus.'

Someone had to ask. I figured it might as well be me.

'Please tell us, Jack, why did they call you Abacus?'

'Because they could count on me.'

Dip snorted with laughter, but Felicity was only interested in one thing.

'What's happening about the doughnuts, then?'

'Well, if it's any use, I shall only be able to manage one,' offered Dip, slipping comfortably into her familiar peacekeeping role. 'Does that help?'

Mark, who had abandoned his attempt to appear desolated by Felicity's lack of trust immediately he saw that it wasn't going to work, tilted his face towards the flaking paintwork of the timbers way above our heads as he considered this new calculation.

'Okay, let's see now, nine divided by five goes one and four over, so Dip has one whole one, and we each get one and four-fifths. Tell you what – if I break one fifth off each doughnut, that'll make nine little fifths, which makes one and four-fifths altogether, and they'll do for you, Flit, won't they?'

'No!' screeched Felicity, biting like the dumbest of dumb fish. 'That's not fair! All I'll end up with is a load of crumbs that Mark's hands have been all over. An' anyway,' she continued, with the passionate earnestness that ten-year-olds so often bring to bear on trivia, 'it doesn't make sense to do it like that, because if you have nine separate four-fifths of a doughnut for four people to have one and four-fifths each out of, that means that the first person will have to have their four-fifths plus another four-fifths plus one-fifth out of the next person's four-fifths, which means that the second person has only got three-fifths, so they'll have to have another four-fifths plus two-fifths out of the next person's four-fifths, so the third person will only have two-fifths left and they'll have to have another four-fifths and three-fifths out of another four-fifths, and that means that the fourth person will –'

'Stop!' I covered my ears with my hands in self-defence. 'You're worse than the milkgirl.'

'But, Mummy!' Felicity was literally in tears. 'It's not fair if Mark does what he said. I always end up getting the rubbish 'cause I'm smallest.'

I felt the same wave of incredulous exasperation rising within me in response to what Felicity was saying as I had so often in reacting to Mark. It seemed to me all wrong that Felicity should get this worked up about nothing. The greatest tragedy she had ever faced in her life was the death of Mario. Blasted kids!

'Felicity, I really cannot understand you. We come out for the afternoon as a family to have a nice time, you've had a go on your blades, and you're about to have a go on the machines in the – the thingy – the arcade in a minute, and now you're crying your eyes out because you don't like the way the doughnuts are being shared out. It's all a complete mystery to me. It really is. I don't know why we bother at all.'

'Mum!' Mark, of all people, obviously felt my reaction was way over the top. 'She only meant about the doughnuts. Anyway, it was my fault – I was only joking, Flit. You can have a whole one and a nearly whole one, darlin'.'

I don't believe my children sometimes. This not only brought the sun out again on Felicity's tear-streaked face, but it also resulted in her throwing her arms around Mark and burying her face affectionately in his chest. Mad, all mad, the whole world mad except for me.

'We might as well have bought the cold ones,' commented Jack, patently bored with these exchanges. 'Is there any danger that we might actually end up eating these doughnuts?'

'Yes,' I said briskly (and sacrificially, because I suddenly wanted to kill them all). 'I only want one as well, so that makes everything much easier, doesn't it?'

'Two each!' Felicity clapped her hands.

'I shan't be having any,' muttered the hitherto famously doughnut-loving Antarctic explorer from a few yards away.

Very well, if that was the way he wanted it.

'Good! Well, if Dad doesn't want any, that'll be – oh, never mind. Give Dip and me ours and take the rest away and fight it out among yourselves. We'll see you in the arcade in a minute.'

After the sacrament of distribution had been completed to the eagle-eyed satisfaction of all concerned, Dip and I followed Mark and Felicity as they set off happily towards the arcade. Jack dropped back to walk beside Mike in order to torture him by eating his two and two-thirds dough-nuts as close to his father's face as he could decently get, and in the most explicitly jammy manner possible.

5

Mark had been absolutely right about the number of people we were likely to find using the amuse-ment arcade at that time on a Sunday afternoon. Coloured lights flashed and winked, snatches of music blared out, buzzers buzzed, moving parts moved, whooshing sounds whooshed and disem-bodied voices repeated their robotic messages over and over again, but at first there appeared to be no human beings around to play on the seductively glittering machines. There were a few people there, though. Strolling slowly through the neon cacophony, we became conscious of shadowy figures moving through dark spaces between the little islands of light, like imps or devils in a portion of hell that had been taken over by the private sector.

We also saw a young man sitting in a windowed, circular booth at the very centre of the arcade. He was one of those heavily built young men who look as if they probably did weight-training with great enthusiasm for a couple of years, then stopped and took up eating as a hobby. After studying him discreetly for a moment, Dip whispered in my ear that his head reminded her of a pudding boiled in a cloth bag, with a face drawn in pencil on the cloth by someone who wasn't very good at art. Mercifully unaware of Dip's bizarrely unflattering assessment, this rare example of pudding-headed man registered our presence with the briefest of dull, unimpressed glances before returning to the limp, lurid-looking magazine that had been occupying his attention. On the counter before him little piles of coins of various values were arranged, presumably for customers who wanted to change larger coins or notes. He and the girl in the doughnut emporium would have walked away with equal first prize in any 'Most Bored Person in the Universe' competition. Idly, I wondered if they knew each other. Perhaps he picked her up every day at the end of the pier when he finished work, and they went off together to do something ever so exciting that had nothing to do with doughnuts or little piles of money. I hoped so. Did this young man know about God? Was he going to hell? Was he was already there …?

'Come on, Mum – we need the dosh!'

Mark's stentorian voice, audible above the whizzing and dinging and mechanical chattering, shattered my holy reverie.

'Let's go, Kathy.' Dip took my arm. 'Time for Money-bags to swing into action again.'

'All right, and then after that shall we come back and win that fellow for the Kingdom with words and exhortations from the Lord?'

'Absolutely not – well, you can.'

'Hm!'

We found Jack, Mark and Felicity, their faces eerily illuminated by glaring artificial light, peering down into a squat, massively heavy-looking edifice of about chest height, with glass panels around the sides and top. Dip and I joined them. Through the glass, in each of six separate but identical cavities around the inside of the machine, a multi-layered pile of two-pence pieces could be seen teetering precipitately on the edge of a shiny metal cliff-face. It seemed impossible for at least some of the coins not to fall.

The idea of the game, as Mark and Felicity attempted to explain simultaneously, was for the person playing to put a two-pence piece through one of the slots in the top of the contraption in such a way that it fell flat in front of a sliding metal bar. This bar shunted the coin forward to a point where it made contact with the rearmost edge of the teetering mass of coins, giving the whole lot a little push which might, hopefully, be sufficient to dislodge some of the coins and send them rattling over the edge into a collection cup, which was directly underneath and accessible from outside. These 'winnings' could then be pocketed or rein-vested by the successful player. Timing was crucial, we gathered. If a coin was placed in the slot at an ill-judged moment, it would lean against the front of the bar when it fell instead of lying flat, and would simply end up being deposited on top of the main pile of two-pence pieces. Also, Mark added, sometimes you had to speculate to accumulate, which smart saying meant that it might be worth sacrificing a few coins in order to gradually push the pile nearer to the edge, the theory being that when the 'avalanche' did occur, you would recoup your outlay and much more. Had we got the idea?

Yes, we had, and I also had the money. I carefully counted three lots of fifty coins into three pairs of eager, outstretched hands, then turned to Dip.

'Have a syndicate, shall we, Dip? Twenty-five coins each alternately into the same slot and share the winnings. What do you say?'

'Suits me,' said Dip. She indicated with her thumb. 'Err, what about Mike?'

Having obviously decided not to register his protest by staying out of the arcade, Mike had trailed in behind us and was parked against a fruit machine a short distance away. With hands pushed deep into his pockets, he had watched morosely while Mark and Felicity struggled to convey the theory of the game, shaking his head in silent disapproval as I took the money out of my bag and placed it into the sweaty palms of my children.

'I don't somehow think he's quite in the mood for a flutter, Dip, but I suppose we ought to give him a chance.' I raised my voice. 'Mike, are you going to come and have a go? Come on – come and let your hair down for once.'

There is a mode of human progress whereby the person in motion manages to convey that, although his or her body is moving closer to you in geometrical terms, their assent to what is happening in your immediate vicinity has actually shifted to a greater distance than before they moved. This, I am sure you will agree, is no mean feat. Mike managed it admirably. Without removing his hands from his pockets, he levered his weight away from the fruit machine with his elbow, and crossed the distance between us with the tragic air of one about to identify the corpse of his best friend. I think he probably had some fairly impressive, doleful line all ready to deliver to us, but, if so, it must have gone right out of his head at the moment when he looked down into the depths of our devil's plaything and saw all those coins hanging over the edge in such mouth-watering profusion. I watched his eyes as they flicked over the money, the slots in the top, the moving bar and the collection cup underneath. He wanted to ask a question, but was wrestling inwardly with the enormous problem of how on earth one could manage to sound disapproving and curious at the same time. I decided to help him out – after all, he had missed out on the doughnuts. His fault entirely, of course, but, as a lifelong sulker myself, I knew what a struggle it would have been to maintain that level of voluntary stupidity. I took him by the arm and pointed.

'Look, Mike, that bar thing pushes the coin when it lands after you drop it in, and makes it push against all the other coins and then you win any that fall in the cup. Good, isn't it?'

Mike studied the set-up for several seconds without moving, then seemed to recollect with a start that he wasn't at all interested.

'I've already made it quite clear,' he said, drawing back, 'that I consider games of this sort to be a waste of –'

'Yyyess!'

A whoop of joy from the other side of the machine, followed by the clink and clatter of what sounded like many coins falling into a metal cup, prevented Mike from concluding a repetition of his earlier homily. Mark's exultant face appeared above the top for an instant, filled with more than Pentecostal ecstasy.

'Loads!' he cried, before ducking away again.

And, inevitably, somewhere lower down beside him, a higher, younger voice said, 'It's not fair!'

'Come on, Kathy,' said Dip, 'let's have a go.'

A part of what Mike had said at lunchtime was right. Something about this machine created or perhaps revealed a surprising depth of sheer old-fashioned greed in me. I found myself quite taken with the thought of all those coins cascading down and overflowing the little cup underneath. I pictured scooping them up in handfuls and filling my bag fatly to the brim. Utter nonsense, of course. Not only did the design of the thing mean that such a quantity of coins was unlikely ever to topple over the edge, but the largest possible win would certainly amount to less than we had brought with us.

Nevertheless, Dip and I had a lot of fun and laughed a great deal, which is worth a couple of quid in my view. Within a few minutes, we were down to about ten coins, despite an occasional dribbling win into our cup, and on the other side of the machine a selection of joyful squeals and shouts, outnumbered by disappointed groans and grunts, suggested that the others were faring in a similar manner. It was as I was about to put the first of those last ten coins into the slot that Mike, who had been standing just behind Dip and me as we played and whose Eeyore-like presence I had temporarily forgotten, poked his head between the two of us and seemed to burst with exasperation.

'Kathy, can't you see you're putting them in all wrong! You're missing it by about half a second each time. You've got to let it drop a split-second after the bar has pushed forward as far as it goes, so that by the time it gets back the coin's just slithering down in time to lie flat and get pushed forward when the bar moves again. Look, give me some of them – I'll show you what I mean.'

'But, I thought –'

'Just give me some!'

Three coins later, Mike, now fiercely, frowningly concentrated on the game that he had so recently scorned, greeted a mini-waterfall of coins into his cup with a loud 'Huh!' of satisfaction. Flushed with excitement, he turned triumphantly to Dip and me.

'You see! You see! I was right! It's all in judging the intervals. Once you've got that worked out it's only a matter of time before you're bound to win. Watch, Kath! Dip, watch!'

I glanced at Dip over the top of my husband's head as he bowed eagerly to his task once more, and made a face. Obviously our little syndicate had been well and truly taken over. Mike was really motoring now.

'There's a whole big batch over on the side just a hair's breadth from dropping,' he said tensely, sounding like a top surgeon faced with an unusually tricky piece of scalpel-work. 'If I can just make the next one land a little farther to the right, I should be able to ... No, not quite, let's just try again ... No, no, I can see where I'm going wrong. Oh, blast! That can't have been more than about a millimetre out. Blast! Blast! Now, come on ... Damn and blast! Kath, give me some more of those coins, will you. It's only a matter of time now.'

One by one, as they ran out of coins themselves, Jack, Mark and Felicity joined Dip and me to observe Mike's fascinating metamorphosis from sulky, moralizing non-participant to raving loony gambler. Every now and then he would glance over his shoulder with bright, staring eyes, comment fleetingly on how close he was to a big win, then plunge every ounce of himself and his attention back into the fray.

'Don't worry,' whispered Dip, 'he'll have lost it all in a minute and then he'll turn back into a human being again.'

It was a reasonable prediction, but wrong. Just as my stock of two-pence pieces was on the point of running out, there was a loud clattering of coins, and Mike threw his arms up with a wild yell of triumph. Unfortunately, in the excitement of the moment, one of his feet must have slipped from under him, because he fell to the side, ending up with his left hand supporting his weight on the floor, and the other clutching the collection cup, which was in the process of overflowing with his winnings. Still filled with the joy of success, he pulled himself up until, with his face not only level with the cup but very nearly in it, he was able to study the fruits of his labours with chuckling satisfaction.

At this point I became hazily aware that our small group of observers had increased by three or four persons. Looking round and focusing on the faces of the newcomers, I recognized, with a little shock of misgiving, that at least two of these short-haired, respectable-looking men were leading lights in the big House Church that met in a disused factory on the industrial estate near our home. One of them, a man who always insisted on referring to himself as Peter J. Lampert, I knew reasonably well from the monthly inter-church meetings that we'd had through the previous year. He was nice, but very holy.

'Peter J.!' I said conversationally, trying to sound as if we had met in Debenham's, or the post office queue. 'What are you doing here?'

Peter J. seemed reluctant to answer at first. He cleared his throat.

'We've been coming down every other Sunday over the last couple of months,' he said, 'to pray against the evil influence that these tools of

Mammon can undoubtedly have, especially on young children. We think that, err, Christians should be very aware of the dangers of these places …'

His words tailed off, and I followed his eyes as they fixed incredulously once more on the figure of my husband, the only one of us who had not wanted to come into the arcade in the first place, down on his knees, cackling and drooling into a sea of two-pence pieces, apparently offering grovelling worship in the presence of his family at the altar of one of those tools of Mammon that can undoubtedly exert an evil influence – especially on young children.

Monday

1

'Ah, there you are, come along in. Go on through and sit down, and I'll make us a drink. Coffee okay? I've only got to pour it out.'

'Oh, yes, thanks, Simon.'

'You too, Kathy?'

'Lovely, yes, thanks.'

Somewhat chastened by his fall from grace in the amusement arcade on Sunday afternoon, Mike had nevertheless remembered to phone Simon Davenport early on Monday morning to arrange for a discussion at the earliest opportunity about Dip's communion, and Simon had invited us to his house that evening.

I felt quite nervous as Mike and I set out to drive to the other side of town for this important interview. It wasn't that I didn't like or respect Simon. Over several years of belonging to his housegroup I had become quite fond of him, and I really did admire his dogged adherence to the straight and narrow as far as faith and behaviour were concerned. Simon was totally dependable. He just – well, how can I put it? He wasn't the sort of person you would want to get drunk with. Not that I do habitually get drunk with people, or on my own for that matter, it's just that I wouldn't have wanted it to be Simon I got drunk with if I did. Something like that. Oh, dear! God understands what I mean.

Simon certainly had reservations about me. A flicker of wariness passed across his darkly handsome, oddly not quite attractive features almost every time I started to speak during group discussions. This chronic wariness probably dated from the very first housegroup that Mike and I attended. At the time I was going through yet another of my periodical bouts of soul-sickness, this time in connection with what people actually meant when they talked about experiencing God. After a Bible study on the seventh chapter of Romans, or something like that, poor unsuspecting Simon began the discussion by enthusing in statutory fashion about how wonderful it was to experience God working in our lives. As far as I can remember, the conversation that followed went roughly like this. (Doris, Stanley and Janet were also members of the group at the time.)

ME: Excuse me, could I ask a question?

SIMON: (PROBABLY PLEASED TO FIND A NEWCOMER SO KEEN TO SEEK KNOWLEDGE) Yes, of course, fire away.

ME: Well, when you say it's wonderful, what exactly do you mean?

SIMON: (AFTER A PAUSE) What do you mean – what exactly do I mean?

ME: Well, how does it feel?

SIMON: How does it feel?

ME: Yes, how does it feel?

SIMON: How does what feel?

ME: The wonderfulness of God working in your life – how does it feel?

SIMON: (SMILING AND SHRUGGING AFTER ANOTHER SHORT FROWNING PAUSE) It just feels like God working in your life. I'm sorry, I'm afraid I don't quite understand what you're asking.

ME: All right, sorry, perhaps I didn't put it very well. What I'm saying is, if it really is wonderful when God works in your life, you must perceive the wonderfulness somehow – unless you guess it or pretend it or something. Agreed?

SIMON: (WARILY – IT MUST HAVE BEGUN HERE!) Mmmm …

ME: Well, what is that experience of perceiving actually like? What happens? Which emotions do you feel? What goes on?

SIMON: (MILDLY ANNOYED BUT STAYING REASONABLY PATIENT) Look, Kathy – it is Kathy, isn't it?

ME: Kathy, yes, that's right.

SIMON: (AFTER A LITTLE INTERNAL REGROUPING) Kathy, it's a spiritual thing. When God works in your life you appreciate the wonder of his presence and what he's doing in a spiritual way – on a spiritual level.

ME: Oh, I see.

SIMON: Good, now let's –

ME: So, how does that feel?

SIMON: (TEETH GRITTED IN A CHARITABLE SORT OF WAY) It's not a matter of feelings, it's a matter of faith.

ME: I see, so you don't feel anything when God works in your life?

MIKE: Kath, let's just –

DORIS: (REGURGITATING A CHUNK OF UNDIGESTED TEACHING) Feelings are unreliable, you see.

SIMON: (LOOKING RELIEVED) Yes, thank you, Doris. That's right – feelings can be very unreliable. We perceive what God is doing through the eyes of faith.

ME: So, we should ignore feelings? How *are* we aware of God, then?

SIMON: Look, we've got a lot to get through, Kathy, so could we just –

STANLEY: (LEANING FORWARD AND INTERRUPTING) A few years ago our car went wrong – didn't it, Janet?

JANET: Yes, it did. On a Monday.

STANLEY: And we were due to drive up to our daughter's in Stafford on the Tuesday. So, we took the car –

JANET: She was expecting the next month and feeling poorly, you see. It was her second and she'd already had trouble with –

STANLEY: So we took the car into the garage, and the man said it was going to cost a hundred and fifty pounds to put right. Well, we didn't have a hundred and fifty pounds, so we left the car there, and decided to call our daughter in the morning to say we weren't able to go. But in the morning a cheque came in the post that was a repayment of something or other, and it was for exactly a hundred and fifty pounds. (LEANING BACK TRIUMPHANTLY) So, there you are.

ME: There we are. Where are we? What do you mean?

STANLEY: Well, whenever anyone asks us why we believe in God we tell them about when he gave us the money for the car that day.

ME: Okay, so that sort of thing happening to you – the coincidence of the money coming – that's the way you see God moving in your life? But you didn't actually encounter him as such?

JANET: (SLIGHTLY TARTLY, AFTER A BRIEF UPROAR CAUSED BY MY USE OF THE WORD 'COINCIDENCE') It wasn't a coincidence. It was God supplying our needs. That's how we encountered him, and seeing as how you're going on about feelings so much, we *felt* very grateful to him.

MIKE: Kathy, don't you think – ?

ME: (COURTING DEATH) Right – so, the times when you've urgently needed money and it *hasn't* come, you've felt just as grateful, have you, because he's wise enough to know that it would be the wrong thing for you to have and he's graciously not allowed it? (SENSING I'VE GOT A BIT CARRIED AWAY) Look, I don't mean that I don't think God gave you that money when you needed it. I'm sure he did, and I'm glad he did. All I'm asking is – what is this thing we call a relationship with Jesus based on? Do we really only experience God in the form of coincidences – sorry, occasions when our needs are met and we assume it must be God – or do we just know by faith that he's there because he says he is. Or is there something else? Is he like an absent father who loves us, but only ever sends presents in the post and never phones, or is it possible to meet him in some other way?

DORIS: (BRAVELY BUT VAGUELY) We meet him in the scriptures.

ME: Have you met him in the scriptures?

DORIS: (SLIGHTLY UNCERTAINLY) Well, yes …

ME: And how does that feel?

DORIS: (HELPLESSLY) Errrm, sort of warmish.

ME: Aaah! (TO SIMON) So, perhaps that's what you meant when you said that it's wonderful when God works in your life. You meant it feels sort of warmish – is that what you meant?

SIMON: We've wasted enough time on this already …

No wonder the poor bloke became wary. I certainly would have done. And how was he going to react now, when I told him that I believed God was telling us to do something quite unlike anything the group had done before? As we made our way through to the big, comfortable sitting-room where our weekly meetings were usually held, I was still mentally rehearsing my account of what had happened and sternly instructing myself to avoid being flippant at all costs. Unfortunately, something about Simon's dead straight earnestness brought out the very worst in me as far as that sort of thing was concerned, and I knew he hated it.

I was more than a little disconcerted to find another person already firmly ensconced in one of the armchairs when we entered the room, especially when I saw who it was. I could tell from

the anxious glance Mike threw in my direction that
he was no more thrilled than I was. He knew only
too well how I was likely to react.

Eileen Carter was another member of our housegroup. Single, devout and in her early forties, she
seemed to have suffered a partial arrest of development around the age of thirteen as far as clothes,
hair and figure were concerned. Today she was
wearing woollen stockings, a straight plaid kilt with
a big ornamental safety-pin attached to one side,
and one of those stiff blouses that make chain-mail
look like tissue paper. Eileen had the odd habit of
addressing people by their full Christian names,
despite everyone else using the shortened forms.
Over the years she had probably brought me as
near to committing physical violence as anyone I'd
met – except Mark, of course, and occasionally
Mike, but then, I loved Mark and Mike, and I did
not love Eileen Carter. I was not proud of this. An
ongoing desire to inflict injury on a fellow Christian
fell more than a tad short of New Testament
teaching in the area of loving your brothers and
sisters. Eileen had been at the top of my prayer list
for a very long time, and seemed likely to remain
there for the foreseeable future or until God
enabled some radical change to take place in my
attitude to her. I certainly never suspected for one
moment that such a change was planned for this
very evening.

'Eileen!' said Mike brightly, as we plumped
down side by side on the sofa, 'we didn't expect to
see you here. How are you?'

Eileen closed her eyes, smiled without parting her lips and inclined her head gently.

'I'm *fine*, Michael, really fine.' She sounded like a suffering nun with TB in one of those bad films they made in the fifties. I braced myself as she turned her ministering gaze on me. 'Katherine, Simon asked me to come along this evening. I gather you're having a little bit of a valley experience, and it might need some thinking and praying through.'

I drew a deep breath in through my nose and released it again before answering. I wanted to be extremely rude, but this whole thing was for Dip, not for me. I must keep a grip on myself.

'Well, actually, Eileen, it's not me who's going through the, err, valley experience.'

Eileen looked at me from under her brows with knowing eyes. I knew that look. Eileen was quite sure that it was me who was going through this hypothetical blasted valley, and, in any case, she would be very unwilling to admit that she had no idea what it was all about. *Why* had Simon asked her to be here? Apart from anything else, when she stared at me like that I usually over-reacted and ended up sounding so cross that everyone assumed she must have touched the proverbial raw spot. I controlled myself womanfully.

'Eileen, it honestly isn't me we've come round to talk about, and it really is not a little problem. It's a very, very big one, and it's been going on for an awful long time. Simon didn't tell you why we wanted to speak to him?'

'God only deals in big solutions,' said Eileen, twinkling her eyes as she leaned forward and linked her fingers around her knees, 'not big problems.'

Simon came in with a tray of drinks and biscuits at that moment, thank heavens. I was conscious that any peace and good humour I'd arrived with was beginning to drain out at the soles of my boots.

'I hope you thought it was a good idea to ask Eileen to join us,' said our host, smiling brightly in transparent and genuine confidence that we would consider it an excellent notion, 'only she does have quite an insight into these matters, as you know. I was sure we'd all value her input.'

'Oh, yes,' fibbed Mike shamelessly, 'very good idea. Thanks for sparing the time, Eileen.'

In response to pressure from the side of Mike's foot against mine, I did make a valiant effort to express agreement with what he'd said, but the words wouldn't pass through some kind of truth-filtering block in my oesophagus. The elongated, strangled squeak that actually emerged from my mouth followed roughly the same verbal tune as Mike's sentence, but it can't have been very convincing.

'Mmmm ...'

I cleared my throat and forced a positive expression on to my face.

'All I've said to Eileen,' continued Simon, adding one small sugar to his coffee and stirring it as he spoke, 'is more or less what you've told me, that there is a serious problem with – well, you haven't yet said who it is who actually has the problem – and you feel a strong conviction that setting up some kind of special meeting would be very helpful to – to the person concerned. Is that about right, so far as it goes?'

I nodded, then hesitated, unwilling for a moment to lay Dip's inner life out for Eileen to stare at. No, I thought, get on with it, you silly idiot. If there was going to be a service Eileen was bound to be there for it anyway, so it didn't make much difference.

'Yes, that's right, Simon. And the person we're talking about is Dip.' I couldn't help noticing out of the corner of my eye that Eileen was now wearing one of those seraphic 'I knew who it was going to be all the time' smiles on her face, but I did my best to block it out. 'It began when she came round on Saturday. She'd already told me she had something important to say, but I'm afraid I was too busy talking and complaining myself to really pay attention ...'

Simon listened attentively and without interruption to my description of the phone call with Dip, and our conversation in her kitchen afterwards. When I had finished speaking there was silence for a second or two, then Eileen gathered herself together as if about to comment, but was mercifully cut off in mid-gather by Simon raising his hand in a slight but unusually authoritative gesture before breaking the silence himself.

'Thank you very much, Kathy, for passing all that on to us. I can't tell you how sad I am that Dip has had to carry such a terrible burden all on her own for so long. It was really brave of her to let you share it with the housegroup. Please tell her I said that, will you?'

The big brown eyes were moist with sincerity. Good old Simon! I warmed to him as never before. He might be a stuffy old trout some of the time, but his heart was in the right place.

'Thank you,' I said foolishly, sounding like a proud mother whose child has been awarded a good-work certificate. 'Yes – yes, of course I will.'

'And you feel, do you,' went on Simon, 'that a little communion service held here on one of our group nights might be helpful?'

'I think it's more than that, Simon,' put in Mike, bless him. 'It's not just a feeling, you see. Kathy's quite sure God is telling her that Dip would benefit enormously from something like that. She's usually right about these things, and I think we should do it. In fact, I think ideally we'd do it this Thursday.'

A warm wave of gratitude and a chill wave of uncertainty passed through me pretty well simultaneously as Mike spoke. It was very nice of him to say that, but for goodness sake! It all sounded so pompous and presumptuous and toe-curlingly embarrassing. How could God possibly be telling me anything? My mind went back to that first housegroup and my obsessionally incessant questioning about how God actually communicates with men and women. Here, if Simon had been a man with less virtue and more imagination, was an ideal opportunity to get a bit of his own back. *How* had I heard so clearly from God? What was I really talking about? Suddenly I wanted to say it was all a mistake and run home and hide (not for the first time) in the bottom of our big wardrobe, where darkness was more welcome and desirable than Narnia. It had all been in my mind – wishful thinking because I so wanted something to happen for Dip. It was just so much rubbish – all of it. God, the church, prayer, worship and all the rest of the clutter we'd invented or dragged together to make existence on this planet half bearable.

'What exactly would you see as being Elizabeth's role in this special communion service?'

Eileen's forehead was wrinkled with frowning concern. It should have made me feel worse, but as a matter of interest it didn't. Considering how lost and panic-stricken I had felt only a second ago, it seemed to make my mind very clear – oddly clear.

'Dip gave her aborted child a name,' I said calmly. 'She called him David. I think what we need to do is leave a gap somewhere in the service, just before we actually take communion perhaps, so that God can do anything he likes about Dip and David, and Dip can respond to it. We can't plan it any more than that. We'll just have to – to trust.'

Eileen pursed her lips judiciously.

'There are warnings in scripture,' she said slowly, with a sideways look at Simon, 'about the dangers of dabbling in anything that might be said to smack of communication with the dead. I think we should be cautious. Perhaps the sensible way forward would be for some of us to gather around

Elizabeth at the next meeting and simply pray that she will find peace of mind.'

'Perhaps the sensible way forward would be to take a risk,' offered my sweety-pie of a risk-detesting husband. 'If the Holy Spirit intends to do something that will help Dip, I'd rather find out what it was than rush around filling up all the gaps with stuff we vaguely hope is a good idea – don't you agree?'

'Katherine,' queried Eileen, 'may I ask exactly how the Lord spoke to you about these things?'

I sighed. I was going to have to go through this after all, just as I thought I'd managed to avoid it.

'All right, but first of all, please, please believe me when I say I'm not claiming that there's anything special about me at all. If I was God I'd choose someone much better and more sensible and consistent and non-judgmental than me if I was going to say something through them – I honestly would. And I'd be the first to say that I could be totally deluded. Of course I could.' I paused, then said, in the interests of truth, 'But I don't happen to think I am. And I will try to explain what happens. The only problem with trying to describe this sort of thing in words is that it's like – it's like trying to wrap a cat in sheets of tissue-paper. Cats keep changing shape because they're alive, and they strongly object to being wrapped in tissue-paper, and they do their very best to *avoid* being wrapped in tissue-paper. Do you know what I mean?'

Eileen stared uncomprehendingly at me. Oh, dear, not a lot of cat-wrapping in this one's background, I thought. Let's try another angle. I thought for a moment, then went on.

'Eileen, you know how, when you're a child, you don't just believe the things grown-ups tell you – you *know* them. They are *facts*. And they go on being facts even when you've grown up yourself and you find that they weren't really true.'

I noticed that, as well as still looking blank, Eileen had moved her hand slightly so that her fingertips were just touching the Bible on her lap. It was as if she was saying, 'Tell me which verse you base this on, so that I feel safe enough to travel with you, and then it won't matter if I don't understand what you're talking about.'

Burying my head in my hand, I searched for a way to clarify what I was saying.

'Look,' I said, surfacing, 'I'm sure you'll think what I just said sounds silly, and I don't blame you, so I'll give you an example of what I mean. In my head – in my more or less sensible grown-up head – I know perfectly well that it's possible to go and buy a new bicycle pump, right? It's simple. All I have to do is just go up to the bike shop and say what I want and they'll give it to me and I'll pay for it and that's that. I've got a brand new pump. Easy. But the child inside me, the child who grew up in a house where, for years and years, there was hardly enough money to buy food for everyone to live on, let alone any spare money, knows that actually it's not that simple. That child knows for a fact that bicycle pumps come approximately five thousand, nine hundred and fifty-seventh on the list of priorities that need to be bought with the money that is available, and that she's jolly well got to mend the old one, or find the coloured bendy bit that got lost in the garage, or borrow one from the boy next door, because you simply *do not buy new pumps, my girl*! Even now, if I had to go and buy a pump, something in me would say that it just doesn't make sense. Foolish? 'Course it is, but it's true.'

I had another thought, and rattled on.

'You just think, Eileen, what that could mean to someone who, let's say, was sexually abused when she was little. Uncle Bob next door used to tell her that the things he made her do were perfectly all right, and even if she felt a little uneasy about what was going on, she believed him because he was one of the big people who know things. Then, as she grows up, she begins to realize that what happened was a long way from being all right, and she has to look back at all those memories from years ago and see them for what they were. One great big problem for her, though, is that the little girl who believed what Uncle Bob told her still believes – she knows – that it was perfectly all right, and she has an awful long journey to make in her head and her feelings before those two true and opposite facts can come together and make sense. Are you with me?'

She was with me all right, but neither of us were quite in the place where I had thought we were. All my annoyance and impatience with Eileen had melted away to be replaced with a sort of shocked compassion as I read on that crumpled, thirteen-year-old face, like the headline on one of those old yellowed newspapers you find under the floorboards, the clear message that there had once been an Uncle Bob in her life, and that she had never told a living soul about it. If I hadn't already been sitting down I would have gone weak at the knees. What was going on? I hadn't come here for this. I hadn't even finished making my point yet. Mike and Simon appeared to be oblivious to what was happening.

'So, Eileen,' I continued, but with a sort of croaking gentleness that must have been utterly bewildering in contrast with the slightly combative tone I had just been using, 'when I was speaking to Dip on the phone, I was suddenly filled up with that same sort of childlike knowing, as though it had always been there, and the thing I knew was that we ought to – you know, have a communion service and help Dip to overcome the past. But, don't you think –'

I did the previously unthinkable. Moving across to Eileen's chair I sat on the arm so that I could take one of her hands in both of mine. I didn't know where I was going now, but as I'd chickened out and surrendered the navigation to someone else it didn't seem to matter too much.

'Eileen, don't you think it's marvellous that God might have a good plan for Dip, or anybody, for that matter, to sort out some of the bad things that have happened to us in our lives?'

Eileen nodded but said nothing. She knew and I knew that if she opened her mouth at this moment, more than a quarter of a century's worth of grief would demand expression, and it certainly couldn't be allowed to happen in front of two men. I looked at Mike, wide-eyed and with his jaw resting gently in his lap. We were pretty well practised in the giving and interpretation of looks. He came to with a start, picked his jaw up and addressed Simon.

'Err, Simon, I've got an idea that Kath and Eileen want to spend a little bit of time together, if that's all right. Perhaps we could just pop into the other room and, err, do some more talking about this communion – or something.'

Simon blinked and wondered, but they left, and for the next half hour I listened, and said very little. The things that sad little Eileen managed to tell me during those thirty minutes do not need to be recorded here, but it is a matter of heavenly record that, between us, we got through enough tissue to wrap many, many cats.

2

Driving home afterwards, I told Mike a little about Eileen, including my own shame as I now faced the fact that I had determinedly kept her out of my life, other than for the unavoidable hour or two of contact on Thursday evenings. That would have to change. He nodded agreement and told me in return that, during the period of their joint banishment to the grease-free Davenport kitchen, Simon had been unexpectedly enthusiastic about the idea of the communion, which was to happen this coming Thursday, as we had hoped.

'When I say it was unexpected, Kath, I mean I thought he would be a lot more cautious than he was, and need to go and discuss it with the vicar or something before making a final decision, but he didn't. He just said he thought we should really go for it. He opened up quite a bit – saying how he's always longed to see God really healing hurt people, people whose hearts have been broken, people like Eileen – and Dip, of course. And how useless he's felt sometimes because people don't really move on much. He's a bit like me, old Simon, pretty well controlled most of the time. It was good to see a spot of passion in him.'

As we drove on without speaking for a minute or two, a steady rain was beginning to fall. I've always loved being the passenger in a car at night when the heavens are opening outside, feeling protected and cosy and sleepy while someone else takes responsibility.

'Mike,' I said drowsily.

'Yes, Kath?'

'Do you think our car is the only one in the world that does animal impressions?'

'I beg your pardon!'

'Well, for a start, there's the cats' paws.'

Flapping a lazy hand, I pointed out hundreds of little pawmarks on the windscreen made by heavy drops of rain flattened as we drove against the wind.

'Now close your eyes and tell me if the noise our worn out old wipers make on the glass isn't just like sea-lions at feeding time.'

'I think I'll pass on closing my eyes, if that's all right with you,' he said, 'otherwise we shall have the ultimate spiritual experience a bit before our time, but you're right. Perhaps we should get it a variety agent.'

'P'raps it'll do well on one of those talent shows like – *Cars in their Eyes*.'

'Not if it tells jokes like that, it won't.'

'You know, you're a funny bloke, Mike.'

'Am I?'

'Yes, I mean, how can you go from sulking like you did yesterday, to being as grown-up and in-charge as you are at school and like you were tonight?'

'I suppose it's not that different from the sort of people who are – let's say – grumpy and awkward one minute, and loyal and loving the next, do you think?'

I pinched his arm.

'We're lucky to have each other, aren't we, Mike?'

'Well, *you* are – lucky to have me, that is. You really fell on your feet there, didn't you? Yes, we are, Kath, we're very lucky. We must try to remember that when our next argument starts.'

'Perhaps we'll never have another argument.'

'Perhaps pigs will fly.'

'For all you know there's an aircraft somewhere that does a very good pig impression, and –'

'Kathy.'

'Yes?'

'Why don't you just let yourself doze off – I'll wake you when we get home.'

I nestled even more closely into his shoulder.

'Mmmmallright …'

Tuesday

1

I woke on Tuesday remembering that I still hadn't done anything about Joscelyn. I felt really bad about the things I'd said to her on that stinky morning, and it was no use trying to tell myself there had been some lofty prophetic content in the words that I had snapped out. I did actually have a go at convincing myself that there might have been, but it was no good. In some theologically sound sense, I was on my own with this. My little tantrum had been born out of pure impatience and irritability, and I needed to do something about it before the housegroup got together on Thursday for Dip's special meeting.

People who are unfortunate enough to be constructed like me are very good at allowing this sort of thing to hang over every aspect of ordinary existence like the darkest of dark clouds. This has a ridiculously devastating effect on one's sense of perspective. Eternal night falls, like winter in the Arctic Circle. There are no scraps of enjoyable melancholy to be grabbed and indulged in, just sick despair arising from the dismal certainty that there is only one possible remedy, namely to actually do the thing that is causing the despair in the first place. And, of course, the longer you delay the dreadful deed, the more difficult it is to do.

In the end I decided to create an extra stepping-stone for myself by phoning Joscelyn to suggest we meet for coffee in town on Wednesday, but translating even that decision into action was another matter. I spent most of Monday morning after Felicity had gone to school dithering uselessly around the house, hungrily seeking any excuse to put off making the call. I was so afraid that John would answer it and tell me off for upsetting his wife, or that Joscelyn would pick up the phone and announce that she had cancelled all her meetings and magazine-writing commitments because her faith was in rags since hearing from me.

At midday, clean out of excuses, I made myself sit by the phone and pray a little prayer. God must have forgiven me for using him as another aid to procrastination, because immediately after finishing I picked up the phone and dialled Joscelyn's number. Drumming my fingertips nervously on the table beside me, I counted the ringing-tones, just as I had done when I called Dip on the Saturday, telling myself that, this time, I would be generous enough to let it ring ten times before giving up. The silence followed by a buzz followed by a click that you hear when an answering machine is turning itself on usually annoys me intensely – I *hate* speaking to answering machines, leaving a recorded message in response to a recorded message – but on this occasion I punched the air with my free hand like Mark does when his football team scores.

'This is the home of Joscelyn and John Wayne,' announced Joscelyn's resonantly confident, dis-embodied voice – recorded before Saturday, no doubt, I thought guiltily. 'We are not here to take your call at the moment, but we are very grateful to you for taking the trouble to ring us. Please leave a message and your name and number after the long tone, and we will look forward to speaking to you later. Thank you.'

After a series of short beeps the long tone invited me to say something. I stumbled into speech.

'Ah, err, Joscelyn – or John – this is Kathy Robinson here with a message for Joscelyn – I just wondered if we could possibly meet for coffee tomorrow, Joscelyn – Wednesday, I mean, at Wickham's in town around ten-thirty, just to – well, to talk.' Cowardice struck. 'Don't bother phoning back if you can make it. I'll just assume you'll be there. Bye.'

I put the phone down and whooshed with relief. At least I'd *done* something about it now, and nothing else need happen until tomorrow. My philosophy in these matters tends to be mad but effective. The world might end before tomorrow, I told myself, or I might develop a serious illness that will mean I can't be there on Wednesday and the Waynes will have to feel sorry for me, or perhaps John will be attacked and eaten by a lion on his way home from work this afternoon and Joscelyn will have to rearrange our date, or – well, anything might happen. I hummed with the relief of it all as I headed upstairs to make my bed. I was still humming as I answered the phone in the bedroom a couple of minutes later. Why did it never occur to me that it could be Joscelyn returning my call?

'Hello, could I speak to Kathy, please?'

'Joscelyn –'

'Kathy, I'm so sorry I didn't answer your call just now, but I was upstairs – if you know what I mean – and by the time I got down the thing had come on and you'd finished your message. I'm really glad you've called actually, because there is something I have been very much wanting to say to you.'

Joscelyn's voice wasn't at all subdued today. On the contrary, she sounded more confident and buoyant than ever. She certainly didn't give the impression of being cross or resentful. Perhaps she was going to make what they called an assertive response to my attack on her. Best for me to eat a good slice of humble pie before she said anything else, I decided.

'Well, I wanted to say something to you as well, Joscelyn, about the stuff I came out with on the phone on Saturday morning. I had just been through an awful night, but I know that's no excuse, and I really am most terribly –'

'But that's exactly what I wanted to talk to you about, Kathy!'

Oh dear.

'Well, I don't blame you, Joscelyn, I really don't. Please say whatever you want.'

I braced myself.

'Kathy, I want to thank you from the bottom of my heart.'

'To *thank* me?'

'Yes, to thank you for just being so obedient.'

'Being so – ?'

'Thank you, Kathy, for being obedient to God when he told you to say those things to me.'

'But it wasn't –'

'I have to confess that at first I did feel just a little bit upset, but then I realized that, through you, I had actually been given something very special indeed. You were right in what you said, Kathy, and I applaud your courage in being so honest. Apart from anything else, those words you spoke to me have been an enormous inspiration on the professional level. I'm just in the process of finishing a magazine article entitled "Sin and forgiveness – the simple heart of the gospel", and when I do my next After-dinner in a month or so, I shall be placing the story of that phone call of ours at an absolutely central point in my talk – assuming you have no objection of course, Kathy.'

'I don't –'

'I knew you wouldn't. I told John you wouldn't. Kathy, you do know what that phone call has done, don't you?'

Uh-oh! The last nail in the coffin of my lingering hope that God might really have spoken through me on that piscine morning was about to be driven in.

'What's that then, Joscelyn?' I asked resignedly.

'Well, I honestly do feel that through your words God has totally transformed me in the most *amazing* way ...'

2

Later that day, when Mike came home from school, I sat him down at the kitchen table, poured him a cup of tea and told him about my conversation with Joscelyn.

'The whole thing worries me a bit, Mike,' I said. 'I mean, you can bet your life that by the time that Saturday morning telephone conversation gets into one of Joscelyn's talks, it's not going to bear much resemblance to what was actually said. Just think how embarrassing it would be if I went along and crept in at the back one day and heard my side of the conversation coming out with its spiritual content cubed. I feel as if I'm just aiding and abetting her in being deluded and passing on her delusions to everybody else. That can't be right, can it, surely?'

Mike smiled and shook his head.

'I don't think you ought to worry yourself about it too much, Kath. I mean – nothing's really altered, has it? From what you say, Joscelyn feels that her life has been completely changed by the realization that her life has not, in fact, been completely changed on all those occasions when she thought it was completely changed, and that'll last for a while until the next thing comes along, and then her life will be – well, it'll be completely changed again. You've just been part of the pattern for a while, that's all. If it comes to that, I suppose we all behave in patterns, don't we? Joscelyn's is easier to identify than most, that's the only difference. From what I've seen, hardly anybody manages to break out of being what they are in any radical sort of way – always assuming that breaking out is a good idea in the first place. Maybe it isn't.'

I considered this for a moment, absent-mindedly holding my ginger biscuit in my tea for so long that the submerged section melted and disappeared into the depths of the cup.

'Damn! I mean blast! I mean blow!' I fished for bits of soggy biscuit with my spoon as I went on. 'Isn't that a bit of a depressing outlook for Christians, though, Mike? I thought we were supposed to believe that following Jesus changes us – renewing of the inner man, new creature in Christ, and all that stuff. What about all that?' Inspiration struck. 'Paul! What about Paul?'

'What about Paul?'

'Well, he was definitely changed, wasn't he? One minute he's single-mindedly hunting down Christians and killing them, the next minute there's a flash of light, he has his Damascus thing, and not only is he preaching Christ to the gentiles in most of the known world, but he's writing half the New Testament in his spare time without benefit of a word processor. If that isn't a change I'd like to know what is.'

Mike placidly stirred his second cup of tea and dunked a biscuit for precisely the correct length of time.

'Paul, eh? Now there, as it happens, you've chosen an excellent example of what I'm trying to say, and the clue to what I mean is in the way you described Paul before he was converted.'

'It is?'

'Well, what did you call him?'

'Paul?'

You have to stand up to these junior teachers with their infernal focused questioning, you know. Mike ploughed on patiently.

'How did you describe Paul before he was a Christian?'

'I dunno – can't remember. I said he was determined, didn't I?'

'No, what you actually said was that he was single-minded. You said that he single-mindedly hunted down Christians and murdered them, right?'

'Right ...'

'Right, well, now tell me how he set about preaching Christ to the gentiles and all the other things he did.'

I had a distinct feeling that if I played my cards right I was about to be awarded a gold star and a large red tick for good work in the classroom.

'He did it single-mindedly?'

'That's it – exactly! Good. Paul didn't stop being Paul. He just became the best possible version of himself that God was able to make him. King David's another good example – no holds barred, whether it was sin or obedience to God. He was extravagant in everything. Never stopped being the kind of person he was, but the things he applied it to were vastly different. I reckon that for most of us it's actually a sort of spiral thing, isn't it?'

'What's a sort of spiral thing?'

'Christian progress. We move round and round in circles, but, all things being equal, we're also moving upwards, perhaps without even realizing it – see what I mean?'

I nodded slowly.

'Or downwards, presumably.'

'Well, yes, some of us.'

'A bit like those swing-ball games where two of you hit a tennis-ball around on the end of a string trying to make it go up or down, and the winner's the one who gets to the top or the bottom first?'

'Err, yes, perhaps.'

'Right, so, as you are moving round your own idiosyncratic Mike Robinson-type circles – let's say, for instance, in our relationship – there should be lots of minor improvements and adjustments going on as you allow God to direct you upward into being the best possible *you* in relation to me?'

'Precisely! You've got it.'

'A positive accretion, as it were?'

He was really impressed with that. Another gold star, I thought, or possibly even a certificate of merit.

'Well, yes, Kathy, that's a very good way of putting it.'

So innocently, schoolmasterishly happy did Mike appear with the fact that the two of us were having what he fondly imagined to be an intelligent, grown-up discussion without arguing, that I almost let him off the next bit of the conversation – only almost, though.

'Well, can I put in a formal application for a special bit of accretion on the next go round, a few minor improvements and adjustments – only little ones?'

Mike looked as wary as he always did when I forced him to descend from the general to the particular.

'What sort of, err, special bit of accretion were you thinking of?'

'It's to do with all this business of us being a bit more – you know – more romantic. I sometimes wish …'

Mike was looking worried now. I deliberately waited for him to ask me what it was that I sometimes wished, but I could have waited until the millennium. He obviously wasn't going to.

'Come on, Mike, ask me what it is that I sometimes wish.'

'What do you sometimes wish, Kath?'

'Well, you know how you talk to Felicity – I've often wished that you could bring yourself to call me the same as you call her.'

Pause.

'You want me to call you Felicity?'

I suppose he felt he owed it to me after my deliberately dumb 'Paul' answer.

'Mike, I would be much obliged if you could see your way clear to removing that serious, puzzled look from your face immediately. That is one of the most blatant pieces of deliberate not-understanding that I've ever witnessed. Just explain to me why on earth I would find it more romantic to be called by my daughter's name.' I looked at my watch. 'You have two minutes, and your time starts – now!'

Mike smiled ruefully.

'I suppose you're talking about a general sort of – being affectionate, are you?' He thought for a moment. 'But you do know I love you, don't you?'

I shrugged.

'Well, yes, but you used to come out and say it quite a lot when we were younger. I have to prise it out of you these days like a midwife helping a ferret give birth to a giraffe.' Mike blenched at my simile, as I knew he would, but I ignored him. 'Nowadays, you voluntarily saying you love me is an event that comes up about as regularly as Oberammergau.' I sighed theatrically. 'Oh, well, I suppose once every ten years isn't that bad, really. A decade passes very quickly when you know you've got something to look forward to.'

'Oh, come on, Kath, it's not as bad as –'

'I've never really thought properly about this before, but ever since Felicity first came along you seem to have been able to talk to her in ways that you've never ever been able to use with anyone else – certainly not me – well, not since we were first courting, anyway.'

Frowning worriedly and blowing air out through puffed cheeks, Mike pushed his chair back a few inches and folded his arms. I couldn't help smiling for a moment at this little amalgam of blatantly symbolic behaviour. It reminded me (no doubt because of my reference to our courting days) of the time, not long after we had first met and fallen in love in beautiful Durham, when the mild-mannered, inwardly rather intense and self-

165

conscious young man I had fallen for so heavily announced, as we walked back after Morning Prayer at St Nick's one Sunday, that he had been reading a most interesting book on the subject of body language. Extracting it eagerly from the bag in which he was wont also to transport his large, black, coffin-like Bible, he showed me the garishly jacketed volume.

Clearly aimed at the money-spending reading masses by an anthropologist of the popular school, this heavily illustrated tome set out to analyse normal human behaviour and to explain it in the context of survival, conflict strategy and tribal behaviour. Fundamentally, the writer confidently asserted, we humans were nothing more than animals walking on our hind legs, and just about all of our habitual behaviours could be understood and explained in those terms.

That Sunday, as we continued with the latest of our darling dawdles along by the river, Mike explained with enthusiasm that the bit of the book he had found really interesting was the section on attack and defence. According to the writer, when we performed simple actions like folding our arms or crossing our legs, we were actually expressing the fact that we felt threatened in some way. In effect, unconsciously, we were guarding our hearts and our genitals ('other vulnerable areas' was the term that I think Mike used for those unspeakable items at the time) against an aggressor. In the context of modern-day living, people who habitually tied their limbs in knots in this way whenever they were in the company of others were, broadly speaking, likely to be defensive types of men and women, unable or unwilling to be truly vulnerable or to let others in on their lives. Those who felt safe and secure in themselves, on the other hand, had no need to erect these barriers.

Thinking about it, Mike said, he had realized that he did indeed have a depressingly consistent tendency to fold his arms and cross his legs whenever he was in the company of people he didn't know very well. As a Christian, he went on to explain earnestly to me, he was seriously concerned about this. It might give non-Christians the idea that he was not open to their involvement in his life. As a human being he was worried that it might be making him look a nervous idiot. As a result of this two-fold concern he had already begun a campaign of monitoring his own limb-folding activities and counteracting the tendency as soon as it manifested itself.

I felt a rush of relief on hearing all this. At church that morning, and during the coffee time afterwards, I had observed Mike behaving in a seriously odd way, and I had been wondering how to approach the subject with him. Seated next to me during the service he had two or three times performed very strange physical manoeuvres, reminiscent of a mechanical toy rather than a human being. His arms would move into the normal folded position, for instance, then abruptly fly apart, as though a button had been pushed or an electrical contact made. His legs also appeared to have acquired a life of their own, folding and then explosively unfolding every now and then in a dervish-like little dance that bore no relation to what was happening in the upper part of his body.

Sharing a pew for an entire Anglican service with a human windmill who occasionally broke into what would nowadays be called a riverdance had been disconcerting enough, but afterwards, sitting and chatting over coffee with some of the other young people who went to the church, things were worse. It was difficult to decide whether Mike was exhausted, or whether he was revealing a streak of exhibitionism hitherto unsuspected by me or anyone else. Instead of adopting his more or less normal sitting posture, he slumped back in one of the plastic chairs, his arms dangling loosely over the sides, his knees pushed as far apart as the resistance of his trouser fabric would allow. This simian pose was punctuated at unnervingly irregular intervals by enfoldings and eruptions of upper and lower limbs as before, the whole phenomenon suggestive of an actor obsessionally rehearsing the portrayal of death-throes. In fact, of course, Mike was practising the appearance of vulnerability, and finding out just how difficult it really was to stop being yourself when no genuine change has taken place.

My smile turned into a laugh as I remembered the alarmed expression on my future husband's face when I gently informed him in the course of that walk that, far from projecting an image of relaxed vulnerability, his bizarre behaviour was likely to get him sectioned if it continued. He did stop after that, which was just as well, because I couldn't have married him if he hadn't.

'What are you laughing at?'

The arms were still folded.

'Oh, I'm sorry, Mike. I was just remembering when you had that dreadful book in Durham before we got married, remember? The one that made you think you'd put everyone off if you folded your arms or crossed your legs, and I had to tell you –'

'All right, all right!' Unfolding his arms in an impressively smooth and rational manner, Mike smiled sheepishly. 'Of course I remember the stupid book. I don't think I've ever felt such a twit in all my life.'

He pushed his chair up to the table again and we sat in silence for a while. I was remembering lots of other things to do with being in Durham. I'm sure he was as well.

'You call her "sweetheart" and "darling" and "love" and – and things like that.'

'Do I?'

'You know you do.'

Looking down into the remnants of his tea, Mike held the end of a teaspoon between the very tips of his finger and thumb, letting it make little dinging noises as it dangled against the inside of the china cup.

'I suppose,' he said slowly and thoughtfully, 'it's all about confidence. Having Felicity is the first time in my life that I've sort of been in charge of a relationship with a female right from the beginning. I know she's not far off swapping roles now that she's reached the ripe old age of ten, but I've been rather pleased – proud, in a funny sort of way – that I've been able to call her those things. It's nice.' He looked up. 'It doesn't matter, does it?'

'Good heavens, no, I didn't mean that. I love the relationship you have with her, I really do. It's just that …'

'You wish I'd say the same things to you.'

'Mmm … I feel silly now.'

'Well, I'll try. It might sound a bit forced at first – sweetheart.'

We both burst into laughter. It sounded ridiculous and unnatural, but I knew Mike. He wouldn't give up now that he'd said he was going to try. For a moment the thought of how the rest of the family were going to enjoy this for all the wrong reasons made me wish I'd never said anything. Still, perhaps it would become more natural with practice, and it was nice …

'Come and sit here, Kath.'

Dropping his spoon into his cup and swinging his knees away from the table, Mike patted his lap invitingly. Gosh, I thought, there's nothing like memories of Durham for shifting the old passion up a gear. I thought about those days again as I cuddled up to him.

'We never did do it before we got married, did we, Mike?'

'Never did do what?'

I groaned.

He smiled and shook his head.

'Sorry – no, we didn't. We were very good, weren't we, Kath? Good Christian young people, that's what we were.'

'We wouldn't have been if I'd had my way, though, would we? I suppose I was potentially a bit of a trollop when it came to it, wasn't I? Do you remember after we got engaged, me going on and on about how we were going to get married anyway, so what difference would it make? And you used to say, all serious, that of course you wanted to do it, but the Bible made it quite clear that we should wait until we were married. Remember?'

'Of course I remember – I still think that.'

'You were so *stern* and responsible.'

'Hmm …'

I tilted my head and looked up at the abashed expression on his face.

'What?'

'I was just thinking, Kath, that actually – what was it Oscar Wilde said?'

Our treasured large tomes of collected writings, essential to dedicated kitchen-dwellers, lived on a shelf high on the long side-wall opposite the table. Raising an arm I waved it in the direction of the complete works of O. Wilde.

'All that.'

'No, I mean, what was it he said epigrammatically about people using what they ought to do or not do as an excuse for not doing or doing something that they actually don't want to do because they're too frightened?'

'I'm not sure, but something tells me he put it a little more concisely than that. You should have married the milkgirl.'

'I wouldn't have minded, she's rather pretty. He did put it better than that. Wait a minute – I've got it! I remember what it was. "Conscience is oft misnamed cowardice."'

'"Conscience is oft misnamed cowardice", eh?' I rolled the thought round my mind. 'I get it – so, what you're saying is that it wasn't so much the teaching of the Bible that was stopping you as cold feet, but you didn't want to admit that, so you got all high and mighty and moral? You were a fraud, Michael Robinson.'

'Well, I was a bit, I suppose. Nervous about being a lousy lover, and worried about doing something I thought was wrong. Ah, well, God does use whatever he can to sort things out, doesn't he? And it's not as if I didn't believe what I was saying. Anyway, whatever the reason, I'm glad now that we didn't sleep together before we got married, aren't you?'

I thought about this, and nodded slowly.

'Yes, I am – I wasn't at all then – but I am glad now.'

'What are you glad about, Mummy?'

So absorbed had we been in our conversation that neither of us had registered the sound of the front door opening and closing. As usual, Felicity slam-dunked the accoutrements of her school life on to one end of the kitchen table and collapsed into a chair as if she had just emerged from eight hours at the coalface instead of a forty-five-minute netball practice. She knitted her brows.

'Why are you sitting on Daddy's lap, Mummy, and what are you glad about?'

'I'm sitting on Daddy's lap because I *like* sitting on Daddy's lap, and I'm gla-a-ad about something else I was talking to Daddy about. Can I get you a drink, darling? Did you have a good day at school? Looking forward to your week off?'

Felicity knew she was being fobbed off, but, as an experienced ten-year-old, she also knew that allowing yourself to be fobbed off without making a fuss has solid commercial value in the parent/child market-place.

'Yes, I am. Can you make me a hot chocolate, and can I go and get the news things from upstairs that me and Jack were doing on Saturday that you never heard, an' read them to you?'

'What a good idea, darling – are you thinking of getting changed while you're up there?' enquired Mike pleasantly.

Parents are delightfully naive sometimes. How could Mike, who deals with kids all day and every day, have so easily forgotten that commands phrased as questions are almost always wasted on intelligent children.

'No,' replied Felicity, precisely echoing her father's pleasant tones, 'I'm not. I'm thinking of doing it afterwards.'

A few minutes later, unchanged, and with her hot chocolate steaming in front of her, Felicity read with occasional stumbles from a sheet of Jack's computer paper.

'Right – here is the news. This week historians announced that the story of Goldilocks we usually hear is wrong. Recent research shows that in the real story, the porridge Goldilocks ate in the cottage belonged to her great-great-grandfather, her great-great-grandmother, her great-grandfather and her great-grandmother. So the story should actually have been called "Goldilocks and the Forebears".'

We tittered dutifully.

'Why is that funny?' asked Felicity, looking up.

'Well, it's – I'll explain later,' said Mike. 'Go on to the next bit.'

'Right, the next one is about a man who was killed in his cottage in the country. Do you think that's good news or bad news?'

'It sounds like bad news,' suggested Mike warily.

'But he died with a huge beam on his face.'

'Oh, well, that's quite good news, isn't it?'

'No, it's not, because the huge beam was part of the cottage ceiling that fell on his head.'

Mike's protest, 'But that's just horrible!' was completely lost on our young newsreader, who had gone off into fits of laughter over the black humour of her second story. I waited for her to recover.

'Is that it, then, sweetheart? Any more ghastly tales for us?'

Felicity sipped her chocolate expertly without lifting it, waving her hand wildly as she did so to signal that we should stay put.

'No, the next one's about you and Mark, Mummy.'

'Oh dear.'

'At ten o'clock yesterday afternoon Mrs Kathy Robinson accompanied her son, Mark Robinson, to the local osteopath, where he was treated for a leg injury. Asked if she had been upset by the visit, Mrs Robinson replied, "No, on the contrary, it was nice to see him being manipulated for a change." I don't understand why that's funny either.'

We did.

Felicity continued.

'Police said today that most crime is committed by petty crooks, and they are just the small-fry. The real big bosses organize everything from inside prison, and they are the stir-fry. Jack's mad. None of these are funny. There's another one about motorways being boring, especially the M6 because it's a major turn-off, and there's one about a man who –'

'That's enough now. Drink your hot chocolate, darling, or it'll get cold.'

'All right.'

A slurp-filled pause. Peace. Mike and I exchanged smiles. Felicity looked up over the top of her mug.

'What were you glad about when I came in, Mummy …?'

Wednesday

1

'Mike, can you write down for us to remember to get a red bulb?'

I have already mentioned the patterns that make up much of family life. I suppose Mike's good old rising spirals are part of that as well, but most of these domestic designs are things you only really recognize when you sit down and think hard about what's happening, or what's happened repeatedly in the past. There are certain such patterns, though, that you can get very worked up about before they even start to appear. More often than not, these are manifested in the form of arguments.

For example (Dip has described this in chilling detail elsewhere), there is the vast gulf that lies between my idea of the best way to pack suitcases for a long journey, and the method favoured by my dear husband. Briefly, mine is chaotic and occupies an evening, whereas Mike's, if anyone was ever plain foolish enough to let him put it into practice, is exceptionally well organized and would take just short of a year. Every time we go away for a family holiday we engage in precisely the same argument in almost exactly the same detail, and it is an argument that has already begun in our hearts, as it were, long before the subject is actually mentioned.

Tonight, I just knew that it was going to be about getting the house cleaned and ready for my party, and the irritation had already begun to seethe around in me as I made coffee in the kitchen to take through to the living-room for Mike and me.

Wednesday evening was our first real chance to plan the party. Jack and Mark had gone out to some pub quiz together, giving us the chance to chat peacefully (that was the theory, anyway) for a couple of hours. Felicity was in, but she had been allowed to choose and rent a video to watch upstairs with her friend, the infamous, high-pitched Caroline Burton, before going to bed. As far as Felicity was concerned, this had not worked out quite as smoothly as it might have done. Caroline's stated preference for films about 'fairies and imps and that' was starkly at variance with our dear daughter's ongoing and so far unsuccessful campaign to persuade us to let her watch a '15', but the one they eventually chose seemed a reasonable compromise, and all was quiet as I set a tray down on the coffee-table in front of Mike at about seven o'clock.

Mike and I think in such different ways. He had equipped himself with a neat little notebook and a new pencil from his special drawer in the bedroom, and would, I am quite sure, have produced a printed agenda if past experience had not taught him that she who constituted the committee was likely to immediately make it into a paper dart and send it on a long-haul flight. I knew that he would be sitting down with a head full of ideas and head-ings and calculations, whereas I had only two things in my head. One was that rising tide of impatience at the thought of our forthcoming, inevitable conflict over getting the house ready, and the other was a determination to make sure that, whatever else we might remember or forget, there must be at least one room in the house on the night of the party that would be lit by a red light-bulb. Hence my opening gambit.

It went down with more of a glug than the *Titanic.* If ever anything was calculated to drive Mike mad with exasperation, it was having random points made at times when a little clear thinking was called for. His sigh sounded as if it was scraping its way over heavy-duty sandpaper.

'Kathy, we'll come to the trivial details in a minute when we've looked at the broad spectrum of what's entailed. I'd really appreciate it if, just for a change, we could discipline ourselves into doing things in some sort of order.'

One of my long-term private ambitions is to creep up behind the broad spectrum of what is entailed, and strangle it.

'What you mean, of course,' I replied grimly, 'is that you'd appreciate it if *I* could discipline *my*self, because, as we all know, you are the most disciplined person on the face of the earth.'

This brief analysis was so palpably true that, although Mike went through all the headshaking, hand-waving, tongue-and-teeth-clicking activity that commonly precedes a denial, he was unable to

actually produce any words to match his panto-
mime. Not that I allowed him much opportunity to
do so if he *had* thought of anything to say.

'I consider myself to be adequately disciplined
in the small but perfectly formed, non-trivial area
of making sure that we have a red light-bulb in one
of the rooms,' I continued coldly. 'I want us to start
with that, and I refuse to talk about anything else
until we've sorted that out, so there!'

I sat back on the sofa and folded my arms.
Being made to feel small brings out the very worst
in me, and has sometimes resulted in clashes of
very heavy artillery between Mike and me.

I shall never forget, for instance, one notable
occasion which was quite decidedly only funny in
retrospect. We had been house-hunting for some
weeks, and the whole tedious process was beginning to get both of us down. Apart from anything
else, it had taken some time to learn the language
of house-selling well enough to translate 'within
easy reach of local transport systems' into 'next to
the lorry depot behind the railway station', and
'enormous potential for development' into 'a
collapsing wreck'. On this typically stressful day I
became increasingly furious with Mike. In our
interminable interviews with estate agents and the
like, he had been tending to take over altogether, as
though he was the adult and I was his little girl who
was obliged to tag along with him, sitting quietly
while the grown-ups attended to their important
business. On the one occasion when I was
graciously permitted to take a leading role, he had

interrupted and qualified the things I said to such an extent that he might as well have done all the talking in the first place. By the time we reached the fourth or fifth of these glorified brick-merchants there was murder in my heart, and, knowing this, Mike must have decided that the time had come for me to be appeased in some way.

'Okay, Kathy,' he communicated in an oleaginous whisper, as we sat by one of the desks waiting for someone to get off the phone and be free to see us, 'this one's all yours. You're the boss this time, okay?'

If he hadn't expressed this invitation in such a condescending way, all might have been well. As it was, his words only served to anger me even further. By the time our professionally smiling, classically uniformed estate agent joined us at the desk, I was way past caring what happened. As far as I can recall, I said, in the most natural manner possible, something along the following lines.

'Good morning. This is my husband. He'll be interrupting and correcting me at regular inter-vals in the most infuriating manner possible. I shall seethe but say nothing in front of you, then get very cross with him afterwards. He'll begin by being upset, but end by losing his temper. I shall sulk and there'll be an uneasy tension between us for a few hours. Later, I shall be having trouble remembering quite why I was so hugely justified in being angry, but be sure that I was. By the end of the day practical requirements will have forced us back into talking normally to each other until the next time. How do you do?'

What the poor young man who had sat down in such an estate-agentish manner to interview us might have replied to this must for ever remain a mystery, because at this point Mike stood up and more or less dragged me out into the street. Later, in my mind's eye, I could still see that young man's face with its open mouth and staring eyes, as clearly as if I had taken a snapshot. Mike and I drove home in silence, and I very much fear that the sun went down on our wrath that night. I was quite ashamed afterwards, but, by George, it felt good at the time!

Now, I watched Mike rubbing his eyes heavily as he tried to work out how to deal with the 'Red Bulb' threat.

'All right,' he said at last, with a sort of weary annoyance, 'I will write down "red bulb", if that's what you really want, and then perhaps we can get on. It is your party we're talking about, you know.'

He wrote for a moment, then held the pad up high for me to look at.

'There, you see, I've written it in great big letters right in the very middle of the first page. Now we'll remember it, won't we? Is that sufficient, or did you want me to put my coat on and pop out to the all-night garage and get one before we go any further?'

Sarcasm may be the lowest form of wit, but it can also be the most annoying. And we hadn't even started about the house yet!

'No,' I replied glacially, 'that won't be necessary, thank you. I would hate to think that you were using up so much energy on something so trivial. You want to get on, so let's get on, shall we?'

Mike peered suspiciously at me for a moment, wondering whether he could possibly take my words at face value.

'Very well,' he said, 'well, let's begin with –'

'Mike, I do just want to sort one thing out straight away. We are intending to have the place cleaned and ready for when people actually arrive, aren't we?'

He very slowly closed the notebook and replaced it on the table without taking his eyes from my face.

'Cleaned and – of course we are. What on earth makes you think we wouldn't, Kathy?'

I gestured vaguely with both hands and shrugged.

'Oh, nothing really – just the trivial fact that on every other occasion when we've done anything like this, we've ended up still rushing madly around tidying up even as guests are coming through the door. Just once – just for *once* – couldn't we try to be ready and calm and cool and holding glasses of wine in our hands when the doorbell goes, instead of one of us being in the shower, and coming out on the landing dripping wet and screaming down the stairs that we haven't got a towel, and the other one creating deliberate and inexplicable mayhem in the kitchen just at the very moment when mayhem in the kitchen is the very last thing we need?'

Mike stared.

'Presumably you're talking about *me* creating mayhem in the kitchen, are you?'

'Well, it's unlikely to be me, isn't it? You must admit I am usefully superficial enough to appreciate the need to do a swift manicure on the house on these occasions, using any cheating shortcuts I can, for the very trivial reason that our visitors might prefer to walk straight into a pleasant environment.'

'Oh, I see, and what is it that I do?'

'What is it that you do? Well, let's see now.'

I settled back and prepared to indulge myself a little.

'For an occasion like this, Michael, your first move would probably be to climb up into the loft and give the purlins and the joists and the rafters a really good scrub, all ready for no one at all to go up there during the party. Then you'd haul our bed right out and clean under that, just in case one of the guests decides he's unwilling to commit his nice clean coat to the top of a bed that might have a thin layer of dust underneath it. Oh, then there's the gutters and the drains! I forgot about the gutters and the drains. Of course, you'd have to clear all the gutters and make sure whatever goes into them can run away easily, so that if, in the course of the evening, someone from our party finds him or herself on the roof – as may well happen, let's face it – and urgently needs to deposit something or other into the gutter, they can do it without worrying.

'What next? Well, *up* with all the floor-coverings,

wash the floorboards, hoover the underside of the carpets, and take the wallpaper off – very carefully, of course – so that you can wipe the walls before sticking it back up. And, of course, it goes without saying that, before doing any of these things, you would have popped up to work and completely tidied and polished your office, so that if the subject of school comes up at the party you'll be able to discuss it without suffering from the nagging feeling that you would be ashamed for whoever you were chatting with to see it if they were there instead of here. What else …?'

'I have never been able to understand,' said Mike with severe dignity, 'why you insist on regarding my preference for carrying work out carefully and in order as some kind of vice. Come on – you tell me. What exactly is wrong with doing things properly?'

'Doing things properly? Doing things *properly*? Is that what you call the way you behave? Mike, you make Hercule Poirot look like – like Sir Les Patterson. You're so maddeningly, infuriatingly, immovably *thorough* in all that you so perfectly do! You remind me of that man in the Ray Bradbury story – remember? Remember the man who'd burgled a house or something, and before leaving he decided to make sure he hadn't left any fingerprints? So he went round with a cloth wiping every surface that he might have been in contact with, but he got obsessional about it, and ended up polishing the underside of some fruit in a bowl that he hadn't even touched, and when the police came he was still in the house cleaning away like a loony, so he got caught. Remember?'

Mike nodded his head laboriously as though it had trebled in weight.

'Yes, I remember the story very well, and it has absolutely nothing to do with how I am. I just don't like being –'

'Cosmetic? Is that the word you're groping for?'

'You didn't give me any time to grope for –'

'If it is, you're absolutely right, because that's exactly what you don't like being. You don't like being cosmetic. You will not do a cosmetic job on anything, and you think it doesn't matter because you're going to know deep down that, even if you haven't got round to such petty trifles as the way things actually look, you've been *thorough*, so it doesn't matter what anyone else thinks. It's a matter of inner integrity. Am I right?'

'Forgive me, I'll make a special effort to be more shallow in future. Kathy, may I ask once again why you seem to be going out of your way to pick a fight when all we're doing is trying to organize *your* party – *sweetheart*?'

I clamped my lips shut and punched downward at the seat on either side of me with clenched fists. I wanted to find a way to tell myself that Mike was being unfair, but I knew he was right. I had deliberately picked the fight that I was sure we were going to end up having anyway. My eyes fell on Mike's closed notebook, never used before, with the words 'KATH'S PARTY' written neatly across the top of the cover, and his shiny new green pencil, both lying neatly on the table between us, and I remembered how much I loved him. I bit my lip. I've been biting my lip like that since I was two years old.

'Mike, I'd really like to start again and ...'

'Kath, I'm sorry I was sarcastic about ...'

I don't know if Mike's thought processes had been similar to mine, but they produced more or less the same result at exactly the same moment. We both laughed.

'You go ahead, Kath.'

'No, you say what you were going to say – I'm really sorry I got so het up. I don't know why I do it. I think it's just that I get all nervy waiting for us to lock horns, and I try to – sort of hurry it along, so we can get on with it and get it over with. Go on, you say what you were going to say.'

Mike leaned forward, opened his notebook, and tore off the first page, the one on which he had written 'LIGHT-BULB' in such risibly huge letters. On the next page he wrote it again, but in proper-sized letters, next to a neat number one in a circle.

'Right – item one in our discussion concerns the need for a red light-bulb to be purchased, said bulb to be employed throughout forthcoming party in the – hold on a minute, Kath, darling, just a small detail, where are we going to put this red bulb and what's it for?'

He called me darling!

'Oh, Mike, you can't have forgotten the red lights they always had at parties when we were in our teens. There was always at least one room where the lighting made everyone look as if they'd just done something they were really ashamed of – come to think of it, they probably had, when I think of some of the parties I went to. Anyway, that's all it was. I'd like there to be one room where I can get lost in David Bowie and dance badly with you in the middle of a crowd of people who all look red in the face. It's important to me.'

'Okay,' said Mike equably, 'it shall be done. Now you've got to tell me what you were going to say.'

'I was going to say that I wanted us to start again and see – just see – if we could talk about what I got all upset about without either of us getting as upset as we usually get. I think Oscar Wilde would have put that better as well, wouldn't he?'

'Look, you tell me calmly and clearly what it is that you want to change about the way I go about doing this party.'

'Clearly and calmly?'

'Yes, and I'll listen without interrupting.'

'Goodness! This is rather like one of those moments in *2001* when the stone pillar comes shooting up out of the ground, isn't it? I'm going to be clear and calm, and you're going to listen without interrupting. A new era has dawned.'

'A new day will have dawned if we don't get on with it, Kath. We've still got a number of important rows to get through tonight, and we've only had one so far. That was a joke, by the way.'

'Oh, good, I'm glad it was a joke, because just for one itsy-bitsy moment I did wonder if it might possibly have been a deliberately inflammatory comment, and that would have been a shame, wouldn't it, darling?'

'Absolutely not, dear sweet light of my life. Shall I open a bottle of wine?'

Armed with a glass each of the heavy, dark, blackcurranty wine that we both enjoyed so much, the evening seemed set to move into a different and more interesting gear altogether, but I was committed to my clear, calm, adult explanation.

'All it is, Mike,' I said, trying to express myself in a clear, calm, adult manner, but probably sounding more like a reception teacher addressing her new intake on their first day, 'is that sometimes, when we've done this sort of thing before, and you've been in charge of the food as usual, we seem to have ended up with you still doing things in the kitchen right up to the very last moment, because you've been so busy – and rightly so, of course, I hasten to add – making sure that the house is nice and clean and tidy – darling.'

There was a pause while Mike checked that he wouldn't be interrupting.

'Right,' he said practically, 'if that's the problem, I think I can suggest an answer. I'll simply adjust my timetable so that I'm aiming to have everything finished an hour before the party starts. If we invite people to come at, say, seven-thirty, then I'll – we'll – make sure everything's completely done by half-past six. How would that be?'

I winked extravagantly, like a pirate, and said, 'That'll be just fine, cap'n, just fine!'

And who could tell? Perhaps it would.

Mike *so* loved being able to write down in his beautiful little book that the party was going to start at seven-thirty. You could see him thinking, 'Good, we've made a start at last.' This is a man, I thought, as I watched his tongue-between-the-teeth concentration, who must once have been a little boy who loved doing his homework and handing it in the next day.

After that we really got on with it, and the further down the bottle we went – I mean, of course, the more we went into responsibly considered issues – the more truly excited I began to feel about celebrating my advanced age. And I must say it was lovely sitting there with Mike, talking earnestly about what we were going to do and how we were going to do it – just being us, warm and together. No doubt the party itself would turn out to be wonderful, but I enjoyed that hour or two of planning as much as I was likely to ever enjoy anything.

You know, there are times when I really do fancy my husband.

Details? Well, the music pretty well decided itself. As well as all the prodigious best of David Bowie, we would have Elvis, the Beatles, the Stones, Bob Dylan, the Everly Brothers (no Cilla Black – surprise, surprise!) and any other obviously significant items of sixties musical culture that we could borrow or find in our own collection.

We decided to have lots and lots of food, which would be laid out on the table in our big kitchen, sufficient to avoid the normal phenomenon of latecomers picking dismally through left-over crumbs and crusts and bits of fatty ham. Folk were certain to bring lots of bottles of this and that, but we would get in a reasonable amount of wine and beer ourselves and put it somewhere at a good distance from the food, together with plenty of soft drinks for drivers, non-imbibers and weaker brothers and sisters.

'And,' proposed Mike, 'as well as all the people we've already asked, let's invite just about anybody else we can think of, apart from one or two of your killer relatives, otherwise we're sure to miss somebody important out and they'll hear about it afterwards and be upset.'

I agreed with him. Apart from anything else, that would ensure that the house was as packed with bodies as it needed to be to create a genuinely chaotic sixties atmosphere. At the same time, we could create extra space for people who didn't want to be crushed to death, by using the whole three storeys of the house – even Mark's room, I suggested, assuming that it could be fumigated and exorcized in the short time remaining to us.

I really was beginning to feel quite excited.

2

Later, after Caroline had gone home and Felicity was safely tucked up in bed, Mark and Jack rolled in, very slightly the worse for wear. Jack collapsed bonelessly on the other end of the settee while

Mark parked himself on the floor in front of the television.

'Got it all sussed, Mumsy?'

Jack's voice was mellow and sleepy.

'Yes, we haven't done at all badly, have we, Mike? We were saying earlier that we'd quite like – Mark, don't turn the telly on, I want to ask you something.'

'It's *Frasier*. I'm leaving the sound down.'

'No you're not. You can't just walk in and change the whole atmosphere. You've had the sort of evening you wanted out there somewhere, but we're still having ours. Turn it right off, please.'

'How do you know I've had the sort of evening I wanted. I might have had a rotten time – you don't know. Why do you always think you know about me?'

Not for the first time, I reflected on the fact that I was rarely allowed any credit by Mark. Cash on the table seemed to be his unvarying terms as far as our relationship was concerned. Very good things that had happened in the same week, or the day before, or even on the same day, very seldom retained enough of their benign influence to temper his response to me on occasions like this. How could he *possibly* think that it was all right to be that rude and spoil the end of our evening?

'Please turn it off, Mark,' said Mike, his voice tinged with a combination of warmth and respect that I had never been able to manage in dealing with my middle child.

Sighing heavily, Mark leaned forward to turn off the television, then turned to face us, drawing his knees up under his chin and wrapping his arms around his legs.

'What? We came second, by the way.'

'Thank you. Congratulations. What was the prize?'

'Beer.'

'We just wanted to ask you if it would be all right for us to use your room for the party. We're going to have loads of people here, so we need all the space we can get. What do you think?'

'Course,' shrugged Mark, somewhat anticlimactically. 'No problem. Might have to give it a bit of a tidy.'

'A bit of a tidy!' Jack flung a lazy arm over the back of the sofa and guffawed spontaneously at this masterpiece of understatement. 'Tell you what,' he said, 'why not leave it as it is and make it into a party game where people have to guess whose room it is, like *Through the Keyhole* where the bloke with the funny voice goes round people's houses?'

He continued with a passable imitation of Loyd Grossman's drawling tones.

'Who would live in a room like this? Let's take a look at the evidence – the stack of three-day-old unwashed dinner-plates with bits of bacon-rind stuck in congealed tomato sauce, the empty beer cans stacked in a pyramid on the windowsill, the ankle-deep layer of stale socks and underwear on the floor, the loose CDs that might have been used as frisbees, the lights and television that are always left on when the owner's out in case someone happens to pop in, the half-drunk mugs of coffee covered in green mould, the bed that Big Daddy and Giant Haystacks have wrestled on for an hour. What kind of person *would* be prepared to live in a room like this? Party guests, it's over to you!'

'I might remind you, Jack,' commented Mike mildly, 'that there was a time just a few years ago when your room was more often than not a forest of empty milk bottles.'

'Anyway, my room's not all that bad,' grinned Mark, completely unabashed by his brother's comments. 'At least I'm better at cleaning my room than Jack is at impressions. Can my friends come to the party, Dad?'

'Ask your mother. It's her birthday party, not mine.'

'Can they, Mum? Pretend you're not cross with me.'

Two options remained. I could grab the nearest heavy object and batter him to death, or I could take the very unusual step of getting down on the floor to tickle him.

You should have heard him scream …

Thursday

1

Shortly after eight o'clock on Thursday evening, I found myself saying a private prayer of gratitude for the way in which Simon Davenport had set up this difficult meeting with such sensitivity. From the offset he established an ideal atmosphere of hushed reverence and expectation very simply and effectively, by his manner as he welcomed people at the door and showed them through to the meeting. He had got the lighting in his living-room just right as well. Apart from a large candle burning in the middle of the coffee table, the only other light source was a small adjustable lamp, placed on a shelf at shoulder level behind Simon and Mike, so that they could see to lead and speak. I could feel the relief in Dip, sitting tensely beside me on the sofa, that whatever happened would happen in near-darkness.

Most of our Bible study group were there, thirteen people in all, including Joscelyn without John (guilty relief!), and Eileen, who was sitting on my other side. Eileen had rung me up on the Tuesday to ask if I thought her new wish to grapple with the past might also be mentioned during the communion service. After a brief and extremely childish wrestling match with God over the fact that it was supposed to be 'Dip's Meeting' – he won by two falls and a submission, by the way – I rang Simon to pass on Eileen's request, and he agreed immediately.

Fortunately, Simon had taken the time and trouble earlier in the week to make sure that every member of the group knew, more or less, why we were having this special communion, so embarrassing explanations were unnecessary. After a brief welcome and introduction, the service began with quite a long period of silence, which Simon said should be used to reflect on the fact that Jesus was with us, as clear and in control as he had ever been when he walked the earth two thousand years ago, and that his promise of healing for the broken-hearted was one that would certainly be kept.

I'm not terribly good at silences. In the middle of this one I thought and felt so many things as I gazed, owl-eyed, at the very faintly flickering candle in the centre of our circle.

I began by thinking about the fact that, in my experience, lots of broken-hearted people *didn't* seem to be healed, and suddenly my faith plummeted. Then I thought about the small number of individuals I knew who actually had been given new heart through their walk with Jesus, and I felt ashamed of my doubt. I moved on from there to feeling a shadow of worry as I once again faced the fact that I was the one who had originally suggested the idea of a communion service. Coincidentally, the candle flame did an extra little flicker at that very moment, and I had to stifle a giggle. It was as if the Holy Spirit had borrowed the candle for a second to say, 'Excuse me, *who* originally suggested it?' Finally, I thought about Jesus, my friend, and tears filled my eyes as I silently implored him to allow some lightening of the burdens carried by our mutual friends.

2

By the time Simon began the celebration itself, the air in the room really did seem alive with possibility, and as we moved nearer and nearer to the sharing of bread and wine, the words of the service, so familiar that at other times they had become mere patterns of sound to me, seemed to ring with fresh depth and meaning.

'Almighty God, to whom all hearts are open, all desires known, and from whom no secrets are hidden; cleanse the thoughts of our hearts by the inspiration of your Holy Spirit, that we may perfectly love you ...'

'We have sinned against you, and against our fellow men, in thought and word and deed, through negligence, through weakness, through our own deliberate fault. We are truly sorry ...'

'We believe in one God, the Father, the almighty, maker of heaven and earth, of all that is seen and unseen ...'

'Lord Jesus Christ, only son of the Father, Lord God, Lamb of God, you take away the sins of the world; have mercy on us ...'

After the Gloria, Mike took over.

'Right, I'd like to read you two quite short Bible extracts before I speak for a little while. The first is from one of my favourite chapters of the Old Testament – well, the whole Bible – Isaiah sixty-one.

' "The Spirit of the Sovereign Lord is on me, because the Lord has appointed me to preach good news to the poor. He has sent me to bind up the broken-hearted, to proclaim freedom for the captives, and release from darkness for the prisoners, to proclaim the year of the Lord's favour and the day of vengeance of our God, to comfort all who mourn, and provide for those who grieve in Zion – to bestow on them a crown of beauty instead of ashes, the oil of gladness instead of mourning, and a garment of praise instead of a spirit of despair. They will be called oaks of righteousness, a planting of the Lord for the display of his splendour." '

Pausing, he found another place in his Bible.

'And the second reading is one that quite a bit of the communion service comes from: Luke, chapter twenty-two, verses fourteen to twenty.

' "When the hour came, Jesus and his apostles reclined at the table. And he said to them, 'I have eagerly desired to eat this Passover with you before I suffer. For I tell you, I will not eat it again until it finds fulfilment in the kingdom of God.' After taking the cup, he gave thanks and said, 'Take this and divide it among you. For I tell you I will not drink again of the fruit of the vine until the kingdom of God comes.' And he took bread, gave thanks and broke it, and gave it to them, saying, 'This is my body given for you; do this in remembrance of me.' In the same way, after the supper he took the cup, saying, 'This cup is the new covenant in my blood, which is poured out for you.' "'

Mike closed his Bible and laid it down on the floor by his feet. For a few seconds he said nothing. Someone sitting on the opposite side shivered suddenly, but not with the cold. The whole room felt to me like a gently breathing, living thing, the light from the candle at its heart. When Mike did begin to speak, it was without notes.

'In a moment we shall be saying one of my favourite prayers, the one we call the Prayer of Humble Access. There are two prayers to choose from at that point in the service, and I think they're both beautiful. The slightly less well known of them begins with these words: "Most merciful Lord, your love compels us to come in …"'

'Communion means so much to me – to all of us – and it doesn't really matter whether it's held in a magnificent cathedral or in this very comfortable sitting-room. And it is a sacrament of cosmic extremes, isn't it? So rich and so poor, so vast and so small, so distant and so near, deeply rooted in the past and yet still flowering miraculously in the present, so ineffably mystical and so very ordinary, so sad and so full of joy.

'It struck me, as I was trying to think what I should say this evening, that these latter extremes of sadness and joy are very significant and neces-sary parts of the celebration that we are all about to be part of.

'What could possibly be sad about communion? Well, communion has always been sad for me because it makes me think of Jesus in the upper room, on the same dreadful night that he was betrayed, gazing yearningly round the table at the faces of his friends as they enjoyed a final meal together. I would imagine that parents suffering from terminal illness must feel that same rush of love and pain as they gaze into the faces of their small children, knowing with stomach-lurching certainty, not just that parting is inevitable, but that, in the midst of grieving, their little ones will struggle in vain to understand why the person they loved and needed so much can no longer be with them. I feel so sad for Jesus – for the man God became.

'Communion also makes me sad for the far less worthy but no less important reason that it demands, over and over again, my assent to the proposition that the whole of my world and my ways, negative and positive, must be left with Bible, hymn book and spectacles on my chair as I app-roach to receive the bread and wine – those wonderful, rich, earthy symbols of heavenly, unearned salvation. Yes, his love compels us to come in, but for some of us, there is a little death to die every single time we yield to that compulsion. Like Simon Peter centuries ago, we yet again instinctively move to draw the sword of our own will and attributes, only to feel the gentle but firmly restraining pressure of his hand upon our arm. At that same moment we hear his voice softly telling us that if we cannot come with hands that are as empty of virtues as they are of sins, we cannot come at all.

'The joys of communion? Well, they are certainly not the opposite side of the coin. They are the same side of the same coin, seen with exactly the same eyes, but cleared by the power of the Spirit, able to recognize the stamp of the King, and to perceive the truly inestimable value of what is being put into these empty hands of ours at this very special time. We stand, equals in spiritual poverty, before our heavenly Father, brothers and sisters united in a desire to meet the God of our salvation, ready to bow our heads humbly before him and to say, "Thank you – so much – that we do not have to trust in our own righteousness."

'Now, a little later we're going to offer each other the bread and wine, and we know that there are at least two people here who will find that quite – traumatic, because they are facing really big and difficult issues in their lives after years of trying to push them away and pretending they don't exist. Let me, as humbly as I can, say something very important to you.'

Mike dropped his eyes so that he did not seem to be addressing anyone in particular, and his voice became, if anything, even quieter, but the words remained crystal clear.

'All of us have to face up to and say sorry for the sins we commit in thought and word and deed, things we should have done, and things we shouldn't have done, just as the old Anglican prayer says. But listen – here is a promise for you.

I promise you that God will never, never blame us for the things that are not our fault, and I think that, tonight, he would very much like to say exactly that. Dear Dip, dear Eileen, the things that happened to you all those years ago, the things that have caused you so much pain for such a long time – it's all right, they were not your fault …'

On the sofa beside me, Eileen began to cry softly. On the other side Dip gripped my hand even more tightly, hardly seeming to breathe, let alone make a sound.

'As far as you are able,' continued Mike, 'when the bread and the wine comes to you, by an effort of the will put those terrible things down for just a moment, open your hearts and your hands, and receive the comfort and love of God in the body and blood of his son. It has always been kept safely there for you anyway, earning interest, and whatever has happened in the past, whatever happens now, and regardless of what happens in the future, nothing in heaven or on earth can ever take it away from you. Do it in remembrance of him. Amen.'

Rightly or wrongly, I felt so proud of Mike.

After Simon had actually said the Prayer of Humble Access, he introduced Grumpy Norman's favourite part of the proceedings, the Sharing of the Peace, by saying the following words:

'Christ is our peace. He has reconciled us to God in one body by the cross. We meet in his name and share his peace. The peace of the Lord be always with you.'

'And also with you,' responded the rest of us.

'Let us offer one another a sign of peace.'

Sometimes, when God does something, it takes a moment to catch on, doesn't it? The fact is that, after Simon said that, *nobody moved*. Possibly it was just that no-one wanted to be first, but I don't think so. I believe that it was my cue, and because an imp of narrowness was muttering in my ear, I was a razor's width from missing it.

'Jesus is here now, Dip,' I said, my voice barely rising above a whisper, 'and David is with him, holding his hand. In some way that we can't understand he's done all his growing up and falling over and having his knees kissed better. He's what he would have been, and you can say whatever you need to say to him.'

Huge single tears reflected the candlelight as they rolled slowly down Dip's cheeks. When she licked her lips before speaking I could almost taste the salt.

'David – darling, I always loved you, you know – always. I have always. I've thought about you every single day. I so wish we could have been together. I'm so very sorry that – that it wasn't possible. Thank you, Jesus, for loving him and looking after him for me. Please help me to let this wound heal. I never want the scar to go, but I – I honestly don't think I can stand the pain any more.' She let her head drop on my shoulder like an exhausted child. 'Can't say any more …'

I fear I must be very shallow. As poor little Eileen, her eyes bright with relieved happiness, ministered the symbols of the body and blood of

Jesus to me a few minutes later, I was horrified to find myself wishing that I was receiving them from someone else, someone more substantial. As I sipped the wine, some words of Dip's echoed in my mind.

'You can't measure the value of the post by the quality of the postman.'

Sighing heavily, I told myself and God that I had a very long way to go, and as I turned to offer the wine to Dip, I saw the candle flame flicker once more, almost as though it was nodding in agreement.

Friday

Early the next morning I confessed my awful thought about Eileen to Mike, and I was still ploughing my furrow as he opened the back door to leave for work.

'Christianity is so blinking difficult,' I complained. 'I mean, why can't there be really neat endings to things? How can it be possible that I listened to that excellent talk of yours, and said those things to Dip, and then had such a miserable, half-baked, uncharitable thought about Eileen? I don't like her any more than I did before, you know – just feel very sorry for her. And we both know it's only a matter of time before Mark and I start biting great lumps out of each other again, don't we? How can it make sense that –'

Mike placed his fingers against my lips.

'Kathy, darling,' – good – 'I do in fact know the answers to every single one of your questions, but I haven't time to give them to you now because if I don't go I shall get told off for being late.'

'Who by? You're the headmaster.'

'By God,' said Mike, with mock piety. 'Bye!'

Ten seconds later the front door bell rang. It was Mike.

'I've had an inspiration,' he said. 'I think I have the answer to your questions. It's unrepented sin in your life.'

'What!'

'Unrepented sin. She's at the end of the road and approaching fast. Bye!'

I thumbed my nose at Mike and his unsuccessful attempt at humour as he departed hurriedly, but he was right about this being as good a time as any to make my peace with the girl who delivered our milk.

I really couldn't blame her for being a little wary. When I opened the front door a few minutes later to find her bending over the crate on the step, she let a couple of empties clatter noisily back into their spaces and peered up the stairs with a rich mixture of apprehension and fascination. For all she knew, naked teenagers telling bad jokes were part of our daily routine.

'I'm glad I caught you,' I began, 'only –'

She straightened.

'There's no need to pay anything today, Mrs Robinson, nor tomorrow, because this week I'm having to treat Friday as though it was Tuesday, so that I can catch up on –'

'No, no,' I interrupted hastily, 'it wasn't about paying.'

'Oh,' she said, smiling brightly and twiddling a ringlet between finger and thumb. 'What was it, then?'

'Well, I just wanted to apologize for – for Mark appearing in that state last Saturday.'

She giggled.

'Well, I was a bit s'prised, but I've got two older brothers myself, and they're both mad.'

Passing over this doubtful reassurance, and rubbing my hands up and down my sides in embarrassment, I moved on.

'The other thing I wanted to say to you was that I, err, I'm really, really sorry I was so rude to you that morning. I'd had a bad beginning to the day, but that was no excuse for taking it out on you, so please forgive me.'

She looked at me with wide eyes.

'Honestly, there's nothing to forgive, Mrs Robinson. Honestly. You were just the same as you always are – honestly.'

'Oh. Oh, right.'

We parted with mutual expressions of goodwill, and a promise from her that she would come to my party the next day if she felt brave enough, but I couldn't help feeling that, from my point of view, the encounter had been less than satisfactory. In her eyes, I was a person with a mad son and a consistently irritable manner. Oh well, I reflected as I closed the door and returned to party preparations, God must have decided that all these loose ends were good for my soul.

'Never mind,' I said to the creator of the universe as I set off up the stairs, 'as long as you give me a nice birthday present tomorrow.'

It was a silly prayer, and I didn't really mean it, but I think he must have been listening …

Saturday

1

'The house looks wonderful, Dip. Tell you what –
let's cancel this evening and just sit in the middle of
it and enjoy the weird feeling of being more or less
organized.'

Mike, Dip and I, with unexpectedly energetic
assistance from Jack, had worked hard since early
morning on Saturday, which was my birthday, and
the day of my party. Three of us started at the top of
the house and worked slowly downwards, while
Mike shopped, prepared food and sorted out the
kitchen. Mark, who wasn't working that day, gutted
his own room to the point where it was merely a
disgusting mess, and then agreed to contribute to
the general effort by taking Felicity out for the day
in order to shop, have lunch and go to the cinema,
in that order. He had been allowed to perform this
selfless act of service on the strict condition that he
didn't abandon his little sister in the section of the
cinema where something suitable for her was
showing, while he trotted off happily to watch
Confessions of a Brain-Damaged Wombat.

It was after five o'clock now. All was quiet, the
house looked and felt abnormally clean (even a
trifle museum-like), and I felt so tired that I
couldn't begin to imagine summoning up the

energy to greet and mix with all the people who would be arriving at my party to congratulate me on being fifty while secretly wondering why I looked seventy.

Leaving Jack to beat an honourable retreat to his room to listen to music, Dip and I had finally agreed to ditch our cleaning materials and flop like an old pair of rubber gloves in the kitchen. There was more than ample evidence that Mike had vastly exceeded his promise of the other evening, for not only was the kitchen perfectly clean and completely tidied, but, as far as we could tell, he had managed to prepare and arrange everything in the food line a good *two and a half hours* before the party was due to begin. I was very impressed. Our long kitchen table, lengthened by the addition of a smaller folding table borrowed from the hall, was groaning with heavily laden bowls, baskets and plates, all decently covered over with two large red table-cloths. The slightly unfortunate overall effect of this, enhanced by the positioning of three or four vertical half-baguettes at the 'foot' end, was that of two rather knobbly corpses laid out under a blanket on a mortuary slab.

'Where *is* Mike?' I wondered out loud. 'I haven't seen or heard him for half an hour or so. Did you see him when you came downstairs just now, Dip? Are you going to put the kettle on?'

'I think he went out to get some more drinks or something,' replied Dip vaguely. 'How about if you put the kettle on and I'll actually make it when it boils?'

'You really have got a bit of a blind spot when it comes to understanding what personal Christian service ought to mean, haven't you, Dip?'

'Absolutely right, Kathy,' she nodded sadly, settling back comfortably in her chair as I hauled myself to my feet. 'I am grossly deficient in that area, whereas you – well, awesome is not the word. The joy of caring for others lights you up like a beacon of hope to those of us who dwell miserably in the eternal darkness of greed and grasping self-ishness. Could you get the biscuits out while you're up? Actually, I think Mike said something earlier about getting your present from him to give you at the party, so he might have gone to do that. I don't think he'd mind me telling you that.' She leaned forward. 'Has it struck you, by the way, that everyone who comes tonight is probably going to bring you a card and a present of some sort? We'll have to find a table or something to put them all on, won't we?'

'Oo, you make me feel quite greedy,' I said, shining like the beacon that I was as I put teabags into two mugs and added two sugars to mine. 'I've already had loads of presents from Mike and the kids this morning. Felicity made me a lovely card with fifty kisses all over it, and Jack and Mark got me perfume between them. As for *you* – wasting far too much money on that beautiful thirties lady I was foolish enough to covet out loud when we went to Brighton. I keep sneaking into the bedroom just to prove to myself it's there. And more tonight! I can't believe it. This is turning out to be like the sort of Christmas I used to fantasize about in my fat, avaricious little childhood soul – piles and heaps and mountains of presents, all for *me*. Now you mention it, I really hadn't thought about everyone bringing something. Gosh, how exciting! I'll share them with you, Dip.'

'I'm still enjoying the present I was given on Thursday,' smiled Dip. 'I don't need anything else at the moment.'

The kettle boiled. I filled the two mugs, added milk from the fridge, and took them back to the table. We looked at each other for a few moments without speaking. I badly wanted to know what kind of difference that communion had really made, but it was difficult to find words that didn't sound like a line from a bad soap.

'Dip, do you feel better about – about David?'

Dip gazed into nowhere for a second or two.

'I have been thinking about that,' she said softly, 'and I'll tell you what I was thinking. There are different kinds of pain, aren't there? There's the pain you get in your teeth, for instance. You know how I hate and loathe and detest going to the dentist, Kathy –'

'The one you've got now has been good, hasn't she?'

'Yes, I was just going to say – to be fair, the one I've got now never hurts me. But I just hate it. And whenever I do get toothache the physical pain seems to be doubled by that awful heart-sinking knowledge that there's only one way of dealing with it. So off I go every time full of misery and tension on the day of my appointment, and I have the injection and the filling, or even an extraction, and then I go home and wait for the anaesthetic to wear off. And sometimes – usually – the pain I get then is as bad or even worse than what I was feeling before. The huge difference, though, is that it's the pain of getting better – the pain of healing. The weight of worry and fear has gone, so, given a couple of tablets and a spot of distraction, I can handle it. I know it will fade in the end, you see.'

'And, it's like that with – ?'

'It's not as easy as that, Kathy. I mean, yes, I hope and pray and half think that it is like that with David. I'll be honest. Confronting the whole thing so totally – so specifically – on Thursday evening, well, it was like one great scream of pain without any anaesthetic, and the pain's still here inside me, the same as – well, probably worse than before, when I used all sorts of tricks to deal with it just to survive.' Her eyes misted over a little as she continued. 'But, Kathy, I'm beginning to think it might be different. This feels to me as if it could just be the pain of getting better, of healing. I do feel as if that awful weight has gone from round my neck – so, I'm going to believe it'll be all right. That's what I'm going to do.' She smiled. 'In the meantime, getting ready for your party is the equivalent to at least three paracetamol tablets, so I'm on track, thank God.'

Yes – thank you!

'I'm so pleased, Dip.'

'Err, I'm afraid I do have one little bone to pick with you, though,' said Dip very seriously. 'I wasn't going to mention it, but I'm afraid I really think I have to.'

My heart sank.

'What is it?'

'You've forgotten to get the biscuits out ...'

2

Being ready so early felt very peculiar indeed. By seven fifteen we were all at action stations, but with nothing left to do.

Mike had eventually returned from his under-cover mission at about five thirty, clutching a mysterious-looking package and looking very pleased with himself. He was now sitting calmly in the kitchen listening to *The Carpenters' Greatest Hits* on our little portable stereo and contentedly jotting things in his little notepad.

Jack had retired to the sitting-room with the door closed (to block out *The Carpenters' Greatest Anagram*, as he insisted on calling it for some reason I hadn't worked out yet) doing some last minute sorting-out of a stack of CDs for use during the party.

Mark was upstairs, recovering from a 'well good' outing with his sister, and probably marvelling at the acres of space revealed by the army of giant earth-moving machines that Dip and I had driven through his room earlier in the day.

Felicity was curled up like a hamster, reading a new book in the window ledge on the stairs, every now and then pushing up on to her knees and peering out through the unfrosted pane at the top to see if her friends, Caroline and Jenny, had arrived for their 'friend's mum's party'.

As soon as Mike got back, Dip zoomed off home to make herself beautiful (out with the earth-moving equipment again, I suggested – how we laughed!) and that just left me – me, the reason for it all – roaming restlessly up and down my spotless hall, wondering why we had ever thought it a good idea for me to make myself this vulnerable. In my mind's eye I pictured the vast majority of our guests stepping out of the shower at this very moment, suddenly remembering that they'd forgotten to buy me a present and wondering if they would be able to find something in the garage shop down the road that didn't look as if it had been bought in the garage shop down the road. I could almost hear the conversations:

'How much do you think we ought to go to?'

'Well, it's a fiftieth, so we can't really get away with less than fifteen, can we?'

'Oh, do you reckon? I was thinking more like ten.'

'Let's say no more than twelve fifty, shall we?'

'Okay – bottle of something a bit posh, perhaps – in one of those fancy boxes. Can't go too far wrong with that, can we? Thank God for off-licences, eh?'

'Good idea. And they do cards up at the late shop. They're a bit crap, but at least we'll have got one. Don't forget to bring a pen in the car …'

These unworthy imaginings, based entirely on my own experience, were abruptly interrupted by a ringing on the doorbell. Such a sudden loud noise shattered the unnatural calm that had fallen over our little world, and catapulted every member of the family into action. Mark came thundering down the stairs like a ton of coal, followed and clung to from behind, poultice-style, by Felicity, who must have got so absorbed in her book that she'd forgotten to check the street for a while, while Jack and Mike dead-heated at the end of the hall just as I was opening the front door to admit my first guest.

The fact that this very first guest turned out to be a strange-looking man in a dingy suit standing uneasily on the step holding a large bunch of carrots requires a little explaining.

Daniel Wigley, a member of our church who has been described elsewhere by Dip as 'one of those square-shaped, friendless men who need to shave twice a day but don't', was in his mid-fifties, and without question one of the oddest people we knew. He was one of those folk who fret so hard over how to do the right thing that they almost invariably worry themselves into doing something inappropriate. During his time in our church, Daniel had developed 'taking offence' to the point where it was a multifaceted art form, reaching its (for him) dangerous peak a few years ago, during a period when we were just beginning to get to know him a little better. Mike made one terrible mistake around this very time when he most untypically completely forgot that the whole family, together with Dip, had been invited as honoured and sole guests to Daniel's fiftieth birthday dinner, and we had flown off in blissful ignorance to America for a holiday, leaving Dip to pick up the pieces.

A providential coincidence had just about saved our bacon when it came to the crunch, but ever since that fiasco Mike had worked really hard on his relationship with the other man, to the point where Daniel was now able to actually laugh – or make a strange rasping noise, at least – about his tendency to opt for being upset when people made him feel foolish or inadequate.

Mike had been really clever over one aspect of this. He pointed out to Daniel that when anyone used the phrase 'don't take offence' it sounded as if they were trying to talk someone out of stealing posts and barbed wire. Daniel found this sadly unfunny observation highly amusing, and it became much more than a joke between the two of them. Whenever Mike noticed Daniel starting to get upset about what he imagined someone had said or done to him, he would wink conspiratorially at him, and say, 'Oi, bring that barbed wire back!' It usually worked, probably because Daniel enjoyed the intimacy of sharing a secret – perhaps for the first time in his life.

This, then, was the person who confronted five pairs of Robinson eyes at exactly seven thirty on the evening of my party, and I suppose it was predictable that he should be the only guest who arrived dead on time. It occurred to me that he had probably been waiting outside, just round the corner, checking his watch to make sure that he didn't commit the awful social gaff of turning up thirty seconds early or fifteen seconds late.

My children have been capable of all sorts of appalling things within the bosom of the family, but there has never been any doubt about their compassion for outsiders who struggle painfully with the business of living. They knew about Daniel. That's why they didn't burst into laughter at the sight of the large and leafy bunch of carrots that he was clutching in his hand. The effort required for such control was, however, a fairly sizeable one. We all stared, and then frowned determinedly. A good two seconds must have elapsed before anyone said anything. Mike recovered first.

'Daniel! Welcome, my old mate! You're the very first to arrive. Come on in. Felicity, take Daniel's coat, darling, and put it in –'

'I *know*!' said Felicity, slightly irritably. She had volunteered herself and her two not-yet-arrived friends for the role of official coat depositors some time ago and didn't want telling. 'You don't have to say it, Daddy.'

As I closed the door and Felicity dashed off up the stairs with our visitor's coat, Daniel turned to me and spoke in his deep, fussy voice.

'A very happy birthday to you, Kathy. I was very unsure about what kind of present to bring you, but in the end I decided that on this very special birthday it would be right to give you something that has a great deal of meaning for me.'

Solemnly, he offered me the bunch of carrots. Solemnly, I took it. I was conscious of Jack and Mark hastily turning away at that moment. I wished I could join them.

'Why are carrots so important to you, Daniel?' asked Mike seriously.

'My father grew carrots on our allotment,' said Daniel. 'I helped.'

Poor, sad Daniel.

'Actually, Daniel,' I said, 'it's just occurred to me that a lot of people like to eat pieces of raw carrot at parties. I could slice them up and put them out with some dips. Thanks ever so much.'

He was radiant – in a low wattage sort of way.

Beginnings of parties are so strange, aren't they? I know it is one of the most over-used clichés of all, but people do seem reluctant to come early and be the ones who get the thing stoked up for the ones who come late. After all our preparations and envisionings, the next half hour felt as though we must have made some terrible miscalculation. The only other guests to arrive during that period were Mark's tadpole friends, Jason and Richard, who were so excruciatingly embarrassed by being at *my* party instead of simply visiting their friend as usual that they could hardly breathe. They came and hung about dutifully in the kitchen for a while because I happened to be there slicing Daniel's carrots. Here, they became increasingly purple, and performed a terror-stricken little circular dance, battling continually to gain and regain the coveted status of being 'the one standing with his back to me'. My attempts to strike up conversation with these two resulted in abject failure, but I did try. A major problem was their voices, which seemed to be emerging from faulty tubes that had become much too small and flattened to allow the words to exit properly.

ME: How's the course going, Jason?
JASON: Glub ...
ME: I can't remember which subjects you're doing ...
JASON: Glubber 'n' glubglub ...
ME: Good, good, and how's your mum, Richard? I haven't seen her down at the Centre for a while.
RICHARD: Mnlub. Mnlubberly umbnlub ...
ME: Ah, right, yes, of course ...

Taking pity on them and myself after a couple of these unproductive exchanges, I suggested to Mark that, since nothing much was happening yet, he should take Jason and Richard and a can or two of beer up to his room. I couldn't help giggling to myself as I listened to them shuffling gratefully away along the hall and up the stairs. It was like magic. Two seconds after departing from my abominable presence, Jason and Richard started to turn into human beings again, and the language of earthlings could once more be heard on their lips.

By eight o'clock, with Daniel happily settled down beside Jack in the sitting-room, clicking his fingers with wild lack of rhythm to Bowie's singles collection and probably hoping against hope that no-one else would arrive to stretch his social skills, and Mark and his tadpoles villainously quaffing ale upstairs and wishing exactly the same thing, it really had begun to feel as if world history had probably finished and nothing else was ever going to happen. Even Dip hadn't arrived yet, and I had been expecting her for half an hour.

Just after eight, though, everything changed. They all came. We hardly had time to close the door between one arrival and the next. It was like the electricity coming back after a power cut, when you've forgotten that you left all your appliances switched on. They came thick and fast, did my guests, some thick, some fast, but all bearing gifts and cards and bottles and the odd very welcome dish of this or that to add to Mike's mortuary slab. Fortunately, Felicity's friends, Caroline and Jenny, were in the vanguard of this procession of visitors. I must say that the speed with which they breathlessly but instantly metamorphosed from party guests into cloakroom attendants was very impressive.

It was wonderful, but more than a little over-whelming and embarrassing to find myself so solidly at the centre of attention, kissed and congratulated and plied with presents by an endless succession of friends and relatives coming through the door. Jack took the brightly wrapped parcels and packages of fascinatingly varied sizes and shapes from me as they were presented, carting them through to the sitting-room and piling them, unopened, on a pair of card-tables that Dip had set up in a corner before she left. It seemed a very great privilege that all these kind people had, at the very least, scoured the afore-mentioned local garage shop or off-licence just to find something suitable to give me. (Much later, when I had time to open all my presents with Felicity's excited assistance, I was to repent of these uncharitable assumptions. It was clear that one or two people had been forced as a matter of urgency to make hurried visits to the off-licence, or to search through the strangely focused retail world of road atlases and household coal, but most of those gifts had a lot of love and thought behind them. It made me feel like crying.)

Included in that early spate of guests were Joscelyn and John Wayne. I had, of course, seen Joscelyn on Thursday at Dip's communion, but this was the first time I had seen John since that dreadful telephone conversation with his wife last Saturday. After Joscelyn had enfolded me in her arms and offered effusive greetings and congratu-lations, John gave me a neat hug, then drew his head back and looked me directly in the eyes for just a second or two, with a little smile playing around his lips and one eyebrow slightly raised. In that moment I understood that it was he who had done the hard work in transforming Joscelyn's perception of my plonking discouragement into a sense of God having radically changed her life yet again, and I blushed for shame. Oddly enough, at that moment it also struck me that there was something about small men that was by no means unattractive.

By eight thirty the house felt – no, the house really was – excitingly full of people, noise and music. After an early tendency on the part of our guests to create one congealed block of humanity in the hall and kitchen, we had finally managed to persuade people that it was all right to spread into most of the other rooms, including the dining-room, where item one on Mike's planning list, my beloved red bulb, cast a nostalgic glow over all those who entered, and over the table laden with bottles and glasses that had doubtless attracted many of them.

Some brave souls even investigated Mark's room on the top floor, where, according to reports, they were greeted with polite but subtly repelling cordiality if they were too old and hadn't got any beer, or wildly inclusive enthusiasm if they were youngish and armed with cans. No doubt a little splinter party was well under way up there. Some mother's instinct told me that this extra celebration was not entirely unplanned, but I had already switched my attitude as firmly as possible to a 'not worrying about it' setting.

Popping my head into our room on the first floor at one point, I found a huge heap of coats laid out and arranged on the bed with great care by our industrious door-girls. These three, finding themselves largely redundant as cloakroom attendants after the first big rush, had exited the house through the sitting-room French windows, and, as far as I knew, were now working out dances on the patio. Glancing once more at the pile of coats before turning away to go back downstairs, I thought about what had happened to my friend all those years ago, and prayed fleetingly that this would be a good evening for her.

Good old Dip. She had given me good advice while we were cleaning up earlier – 'don't drink much at your own party' – and she was absolutely right. Mind you, I didn't really want to, anyway. It was intoxicating enough to move from room to room, savouring the fact that the most important people in my life were richly layered together in one place – well, very nearly all the most important people in my life. By nine o'clock I still hadn't seen any sign of Dip, though the place was so packed by now that it was difficult to know who was there and who wasn't. When I mentioned it to Mike he assured me he had seen and talked to her only a few minutes earlier, and anyway, he pointed out, her car was parked directly outside our house at that very moment. I checked, and he was right.

Once or twice, too, right in the middle of laughing and chatting with folk, I had felt a sudden stab of pain about my stupidity in refusing that once-only opportunity to cross the world and be with my brother and his family, but I did my best to push those thoughts away. This was not the night for stabs of pain. This was a night for celebration.

'Sitting-room, everybody! Felicity, can you go right up to the top of the house, please – yes, you do have to, the other two can help you – and tell everyone you meet and everyone you don't meet that they've got to come downstairs. Go on – off you go! Sitting-room, everybody! Time to embarrass Kathy!'

3

There really is no point at all in trying to resist junior headmasters, you know. They expect to be obeyed. The human pools and tributaries that were filling our house began to flow with sluggish obedience down towards the biggest land-locked sea, which was the sitting-room.

Jack steered me firmly in the same direction. On reaching our destination at last, he indicated a little space at the garden end of the room with a high stool in the middle of it, this being the spot where his father's master plan presumably demanded that I should park myself.

I did maintain a more or less appropriate smirk on my face as I sat like a lemon on my stool, watching everyone trying to squeeze into a space that was nowhere near large enough for comfort, but inwardly I was the teeniest bit miffed. It sounds ungrateful, but I had just begun to really enjoy the unstructured bustle and noise of my party. Especially, I had been feeling obscurely flattered by the sight of people engaged in conversation and laughing with each other in our house – in a situation that we had created. Perhaps it was a similar satisfaction to the one felt by those lucky people who write plays and create sets, then watch actors and actresses playing out their dreams like puppets. Probably it was much more childish than that.

'Right, squeeze in everybody,' shouted Mike over the hubbub, 'bring your glass with you or grab another one. Make sure there's something in it. Come on, push up at the front and push in at the back. We don't want anyone to end up gnashing their teeth in the hall.'

I don't know if Mike pictured everyone sitting in neat cross-legged rows with a grown-up on a chair at the end of each line. If so, he must have been sorely disappointed. Shrieks and squeals of hysterical laughter from those who enjoyed this kind of thing accompanied chaotic efforts by all those present to obey Mike's command, but in the end, by some sacrificial, floor-dwelling, lap-sitting, intertwining miracle of limb redistribution, the entire assembly was at last corked tightly into the room, and Mike held up a hand for hush.

'Right, I want to start,' he said, 'by thanking you all very much for your good wishes and your gifts, but thank you most of all for simply being here to help us celebrate Kathy's sixtieth birthday tonight.'

I swung my arm stiffly like one of those entry gates in the supermarket, hitting him jovially but quite firmly with the back of my fist. Much laughter.

'Sorry, Kath, I meant fiftieth, of course. Time passes so quickly when you're having fun – so I've been told.'

More laughter.

'I don't think we've ever had so many friends and family all together at exactly the same time. It really is so lovely to see you all in our home. So, let's start by giving each other a big round of applause for being here at all.'

As people clapped furiously, I scanned the sea of faces before me. The whole world seemed to be squashed into our sitting-room. Jack, Mark and Felicity were sitting on the floor, more or less at my feet. I could sense a very natural excitement in them, but there was an excitement within their excitement that rather puzzled me.

Carefully selected relatives beamed in my direction from various points in the room (they had been selected on the basis of beaming potential and discretion). Simon Davenport was there, as well as Eileen and the rest of our housegroup, together with other friends from the church. The girl who delivered the milk had plucked up her courage and come. There she was now by the door, looking very pretty out of uniform, and happy, if a little confused. Colleagues from Mike's school had come, and folk from the immediate neighbourhood, including the increasingly frail but unquenchably feisty Mrs Van Geeting from next door, a particular across-the-fence favourite with Dip and me. Even Mark's tadpoles were jammed into an impossibly small space in the angle of the wall behind the television in the far corner. Everyone was there, in fact, except – I swept the room with my eyes one more time to make sure – everyone except Dip. She was nowhere to be seen. My heart sank.

'Mike!' I hissed, as the applause began to subside. 'Dip's *not* here. She must have got cold feet. I think we should –'

'Dip's fine,' he interrupted in a whisper, laying a hand on my shoulder. 'Trust me!'

So, after looking into his eyes for a moment, and although it didn't make any sense, I trusted him.

'Okay!' Mike clapped his hands together and rubbed his palms expectantly. 'Our three children are here in front of us, and before I make my little speech they've all got something to say.' Pause. 'I'm very proud of my children –'

'Uh-oh!' I interrupted. 'Joke on the starboard bow – fire at will.'

Cheers from many and machine-gun noises from a few.

'No, no, I mean it. We're glad we had Jack, Mark and Felicity, despite friends advising us early in our marriage that we should avoid having children for the same reason that we shouldn't change our car from petrol to diesel. They told us that, compared with petrol, diesel was noisy, smelly, and lacked acceleration.'

Laughter, groans, the odd cry of 'Shame!' and a disapproving glare from Felicity, who had reached the age where jokes of that sort had to be about other people. Even a light-hearted suggestion that she might be noisy, smelly and slow didn't go down at all well. I directed a reassuring, he-was-only-joking smile at her, but she brightened up anyway at Mike's next words.

'I know that Felicity and Jack have something to

do for you now, so I'll hand you over to them. Jack and Felicity!'

Amid tumultuous, floor-thumping applause, Jack and Felicity got to their feet and stood on either side of me facing the populace, each clutching a sheet of paper.

'Felicity and I would like to perform a sort of tribute to Mum,' announced Jack gravely, as soon as there was quiet.

I sensed everyone gearing up to being deeply moved, but none of them knew Jack as well as I did. I smiled inside and did my level best to look as sombre as my son.

'Yes,' said Felicity with equal gravity, 'we wrote down all the things about Mum that came into both our heads an' turned them into a poem. Well, Jack did most of the turning, but I helped.'

'A serious poem,' added Jack, 'about a person we deeply respect.'

Felicity nodded in earnest agreement, but her whole body was bobbing and quivering infinitesimally with the joy of the moment.

'We're going to read a verse alternatively,' she said.

'Alternately,' corrected Jack.

'Alternately – a verse each at a time.'

'That's right, with Flitty starting.'

The doggerel that my daughter and her oldest brother then proceeded to recite was so heavily punctuated and interrupted by laughter, cat-calls and applause that an accurate record of the event itself is virtually impossible. Here, however, is a bald transcription of the verses that they read:

Mummy lives in Daddy's house,
She gets all red and cross,
She watches *Friends* on telly,
And she really fancies Ross.

Mummy says, 'Be good at meals,'
And shouts when we don't do it,
She picked a bowl of leeks up once,
And jolly nearly threw it.

Mummy does aerobics,
With some younger, thinner mothers,
She wears long shirts and leggings,
And she hides behind the others.

Mummy told her best friend, Dip,
About her favourite dream,
She falls into a river,
And it's made of Bristol Cream.

Born with three-score years and ten,
Of fifty she's bereft,
Or, turned into a fraction,
She's got three-sevenths left.

Mummy was a writer once,
She even wrote a book,
But since the 'blasted kids' arrived,
She's forced to clean and cook.

For almost half her life on earth,
Our mum has loved us best.
Thank you, Mum, we promise,
We will love you for the rest.

There was no doubting the success of this item. Thunderous appreciation threatened to lift the roof off our faithful old centurion of a house, as Felicity, her face flushed with pleasure and pride, threw her arms around my neck, kissed me on the cheek, and wished me a happy birthday.

I had to check a tear at this point, not, as it happens, in response to the last verse of the poem (I knew all too well that my children loved me), but because of the reference to my writing. This reaction took me by surprise. It was not unlike another moment in the recent past when I had become aware that I was no longer mourning my mother's death with the same suffocating pungency of grief as in the early days after losing her. I had felt ashamed of overcoming the worst of my pain, as though I had let her down.

But this was about writing. I had once been a writer. Now I was fifty, and I was not a writer any more. Okay, I accepted it, but what was I? How do you find out what you are?

I hugged Felicity hard, wishing, as I buried my face in the warm material of her sweatshirt, that my mother could be here at my party, fiddling around endlessly in the kitchen, scolding me for getting het up, pointing out what was wrong with my life in private and defending me to the death in public. If

she could have just – been here. All the old God
stuff had jolly well better be right, I thought. I
pulled myself together as Mike spoke again.

'Thank you very much, Jack and Felicity.
Felicity will be –'

'Hey, hold on,' I broke in, 'surely I'm allowed to
say just a word or two in my own defence, aren't I?'

'Mmm, I don't know – well, okay, I'll put it to the
vote,' said Mike. 'All those in favour of Kathy being
allowed to say a word or two in her own defence,
please raise a hand.'

A veritable garden-centre of hands shot up.

'Thank you very much for your kind permis-
sion. First of all, I thought it was an excellent poem,
and very well read – well done, Felicity and Jack.
Having said that, I must insist on salvaging what
remains of my good name and my reputation for
sanity by pointing out that I most certainly do not
fancy Ross. As Jack and Felicity know full well, I
would regard going out with him as the rough
equivalent of marrying my great-aunt. When the
last trump sounds and all is revealed, the communion of saints on earth and in heaven will learn that
his name was only put on the end of the last line
because it rhymes with "cross", an adjective that I
suppose might occasionally be applied to me ...'

Exaggerated gasps of incredulity from all the
members of my immediate family, and from one or
two others present as well.

'As for the bowl of leeks, I deeply resent the
suggestion that I nearly threw it. I *did* throw it –
well, I slid it as hard as I could and it would have

fallen on the floor if Mike hadn't caught it at the other end …'

Riotous applause, received by Mike with a gracious bow, after which I continued.

'It was an extraordinarily satisfying thing to do, and I would thoroughly recommend it to all those whose children react to the sight of their mother's choicer dishes by sticking their fingers in their mouths and pretending to vomit. As for the rest of the poem, the aerobics, the – what was the other thing? – ah, yes, the sherry dream, only having three-sevenths of my life left, and calling this lot 'the blasted kids' on one or two occasions, I confess to them all, but I absolutely refuse to repent, as it's my birthday. Thank you.'

'As I was about to say before I was so predictably interrupted,' continued Mike as soon as calm returned once more, 'Felicity will be doing one other thing a little later on, but I know that Jack and Mark want to say a few words now.'

Jack, still standing beside me, cleared his throat.

'I don't want to say much, just that I love my mum and I hope she has a really good party, and a happy birthday and, most important of all, I hope God forgives her for lying about Ross. Happy birthday, Mumsy.'

The smile he gave me before sitting down was a much better speech. I shook my head in wonder. Imagine my first baby becoming a proper grown-up.

I felt quite worried for Mark as he dragged himself to his feet, his dark features unusually pink and nervous. Secretly I was amazed that he had decided to say anything at all in public. This was certainly not his sort of thing, and it can't have been made any easier by the fact that there was a complete absence of noise as he turned to face the room. It was as if all those people somehow sensed the fragility of his confidence, and were afraid that a slight sound might kill it altogether. When he did start to speak, it was quietly, and definitely in the manner of one who has abandoned his prepared speech.

'Mum an' I don't always get on.'

The silence, into which these seven words fell like sparrows' eggs onto a snowdrift, was made to seem even more profound by a very faint hiccup of ten-year-old satirical laughter from Felicity, who was sitting cross-legged on the floor next to me, staring at her ankles. At the back of the room the tadpoles were transfixed behind the telly, rigid with horror as they imagined themselves committing such an appalling act of self-exposure.

'We are sort of like each other really – well, in ways, you know …'

Mark turned towards me, a fierce frown on his face.

'But, it doesn't mean – I mean, just because we sometimes fall out doesn't mean that we don't – you know. I try an' she tries …'

Oh, Mark …

'Anyway – happy birthday, Mum.'

As Mark put his arms round me and kissed me awkwardly, I realized for the first time what people meant when they talked about 'filling up' with emotion. The cumulative effect of the last few days and the things that were happening this evening was pretty powerful. I wasn't keen to overflow in front of all my guests, but I wasn't sure how long I could hold out.

'Just a couple more things!' Mike raised his voice and flapped his arms to quell the explosion of approval that had greeted Mark's speech. 'Just two more things before we all go and have some food and get on with the party. First of all, I'd like you all to raise your glasses and drink a toast to Kathy. She and I don't always get on either …'

Comfortable laughter.

'But she's still my sweetheart and I really do love her very much. Kath, darling, I wish you the happiest birthday of your whole life. To Kathy!'

'To Kathy!' echoed the assembly, tilting their glasses with gusto, as assemblies do.

'*Just* one more thing.'

Goodness, what now?

Reaching over to one of the present tables, Mike picked up the mysteriously shaped package he had brought home just before the party began, and made a signal to Felicity, who immediately turned and produced her violin and bow from somewhere behind the place where she had been sitting.

'Stand up, sweetheart, that's it. Ready? Good! Now, everybody, the final thing I want to do is give Kathy her birthday present from me. And before I hand it over, Felicity's going to give her a very subtle little musical clue as to what it is. Listen care-fully, Kath. Right, off you go, darling.'

If I live to be a hundred I shall never forget the strangeness of the next minute or so. It says something about my state of mind that, for twenty seconds at least, the name of the very familiar piece of music Felicity started to play escaped me completely. I found myself concentrating intently on my daughter's fingers as they danced on the neck of her instrument, dimly aware that this lilting tune had enormous significance if I could only clear my mind enough to recognize it. At the instant when it finally clicked that, of course, the tune was 'Waltzing Matilda', I felt a sudden rush of cold air from behind me and heard a gasp from one of my relatives at the back of the room. Turning, the only thing my eyes focused on at first was Dip standing by the open French windows, flushed and excited, with what appeared to be the keys of our car dangling from her fingers. I remember frowning in real bewilderment and actually trying to move towards her to ask what was going on, but making no progress at all because I was blocked by a tall stranger in an overcoat, who grabbed my shoulders and tilted my chin so that I was forced to look up into his face. I came near to fainting on the spot when I recognized the barely altered features of the older brother I had feared I would never see again this side of heaven. From somewhere beside me Mike said quietly, 'Happy birthday, darling,' and after that I couldn't stop the tears any more.

Sunday

1

'Come on now, Kathy, be honest. Did you have any idea what was going to happen?'

'Mmm, well, I was a bit puzzled about how the children were. I don't know – they were just that bit more quiveringly excited than you might have expected, given what was going on. And then, when you didn't seem to be around after the party got under way, Dip, well, that was a mystery and a real worry. I suppose it occurred to me there must be *something* in the air, but I honestly and truthfully hadn't the remotest notion that Mike had sorted out the money for Pete to fly over on one of those standby efforts. And at such incredibly short notice, too! The lying rat told me we couldn't afford it any more and I believed him. Apart from anything else, if you remember, he arrived back a couple of hours before the party with what now turns out to be an awkwardly shaped old bit of wood nicely wrapped up in pretty paper, didn't he? All a cover for his nefarious plans. When he picked it up just before Felicity did her bit on the violin I really did think that was what he was about to present me with. Gosh, he was never that good a liar before, Dip. I'm going to have to watch him in future.' I clapped a hand to my head. 'Hold on a minute, what am I saying? You're just as bad, aren't you, my so-called best friend? You've been keeping it under your hat all week.'

Dip tried to look contrite, but succeeded only in looking as smugly pleased with herself as she had done ever since yesterday evening, when she had been personally responsible to Mike for driving to the airport and back (in our car, so that Pete's luggage could be accommodated) to collect, entertain at her house until the right moment, and finally deliver the best birthday present I had ever been given.

It was Sunday afternoon. By mutual consent no-one had been to church that morning. Pete was upstairs (my brother Pete, upstairs in one of *our* rooms, in our house, at that very moment) sleeping the sandbagged sleep of the severely jet-lagged, while Mike had driven the others up on to the hills with their kites on this crisp, breezy day, presumably feeling that an hour or two of intensive unravelling practice would do them good. Dip and I, pleasantly dozy as a result of not getting to bed until the early hours, were sprawled in the sitting-room, relishing the process of reviewing an event that had not only been hugely successful and enjoyable, but, just as importantly, was now safely in the past. Between us we had managed to clear away all unwanted traces of yesterday's celebrations, and now, for an hour or so anyway, there was nothing left to do but relax and natter. Dip leaned forward to take a birthday choco-late and pour a little more sherry into my glass.

'What was your favourite bit of the party?' she asked.

'Apart from your Cilla Black impression, do you mean?'

'I thought it was more like *This Is Your Life* myself. Apart from that, yes.'

I leaned back in my chair and considered for a moment, twirling my glass in my fingers like a posy of flowers as the memory returned.

'Oh, I think it was when I danced with Pete in the red bulb room. The surprise-surprise part was wonderful, of course it was, but it sort of took my breath away, and we were both in tears in any case. But then, when we did that little smooch later on in the dining-room –' I sighed. 'Having Pete there and the whole atmosphere and everything, it seemed to bring so much of the past back with a – a warm whoosh! And I felt *really* happy, Dip. It's reassuring for someone like me to know that it's possible to feel as all right as that, even if it only lasts for a few minutes. Makes you look forward to heaven a bit more. What was your favourite bit?'

Dip turned her head to one side and thought.

'Sharing a secret. Being a small part of making it happen. Seeing your face when it did. Not ending up talking about cloud formations to Daniel for the *entire* evening in the angle of the kitchen doorway. Those were the highlights.'

'Actually, Dip, to be deadly serious for a moment, I think, if you're honest with yourself, the Lord has been telling you for a long time that you should marry Daniel. He's certainly been making it very clear to me.'

'Now, if you meant that,' said Dip sardonically, 'it would be a very good example of what one might call anti-evangelism. Fond as I am of Daniel, if I ever seriously thought the divine will was demanding that we spend the rest of our lives together, I would bend my knee to the nearest available idol and cancel my monthly standing order to the Church of England. Your brother, now – that's another matter. Shame he's married.'

'Mmm, that would've been neat, wouldn't it? Nice foursome we'd have made, eh? Hard luck. By the way, Pete says there's a chance he'll be coming back on business in a couple of years, and they might let him bring Dawn and the girls. Wouldn't that be great? I'd really love it. It's so wonderful to have just him for a little while, though.' I shook my head. 'I still can't get over Mike doing that. Amazing – simply amazing.'

'Those fears of yours about ruining everything when you met – all gone up in a puff of smoke, have they?'

I rolled my shoulders impatiently on the back of the sofa, clicking my tongue in annoyance at the memory of my own foolishness.

'Of course they bloomin' well have, Dip. I don't know how I could have been so stupid. I suppose it was just that it had been so long, and it meant so much to me. I lost confidence and got scared. No, the moment I recognized Pete all that rubbish just – did whatever you said.'

'Went up in smoke?'

'Mm, that's it.'

We sat happily without speaking for a little while. Glancing through the window beside me I saw that the sky had blackened angrily, threatening rain. The kite-flyers would be starting to make their way back by now. An old-fashioned Sunday tea would be nice if we ever managed to stand up again. Inside, the late afternoon gloom of the sitting-room was only faintly relieved by the last of our birch logs flaming and glowing in the grate. It felt to me like the kind of atmosphere in which great thoughts might possibly find expression.

'Bacon,' said Dip solemnly.

'I beg your pardon?'

'I used the word "anti-evangelism" just now. Well, I've just solved the whole problem of how to evangelize really effectively.'

'Using bacon?'

'Yes,' she continued dreamily. 'I don't see how you could go wrong. You set up a huge tent near the middle of the town one day, and when you're ready for the meeting to begin you start frying loads of bacon inside. Then, when the heavenly scent has drawn lots of people in, as it's bound to, you sit them down, preach at them for a while, and then tell them that anyone who makes a commitment can have some bacon, and anyone who doesn't can stay hungry and clear off. Can't fail, can it? I don't understand why no one's tried it before.'

'No, God must be kicking himself for starting the whole movement off in a part of the world where that ploy was unlikely to work. Hmm, I wonder how people like Billy Graham would react to the news that they're potentially slightly less effective than a couple of rashers of unsmoked back?'

'Oh, well, we visionaries have to put up with a lot of misunderstanding and prejudice. We accept that. I gather the kids did really well just before I arrived last night, Kathy?'

'Dip, they were wonderful. I felt as if we were one of those real families you read about in American paperbacks. Mark was especially – oh, I don't know what he especially was, but I wished we could just hold on to that little bit of time and never have any more of our rotten battles. You will pray for Mark and me, won't you?'

She shook her head at my silliness.

'Don't worry. Praying for you and your kids has become almost as much of a habit as breathing, and I wasn't planning to give up either of those essential activities for the next few years.'

I looked at her speculatively.

'And *I* shall pray about what's going to happen for *you* during those next few years. Do you think it's possible that anything – different could be on the cards?'

'Different? What do you mean – different?'

'Oh, you know – different.'

'Well, it's possible,' said Dip, stroking her chin and looking straight at me, 'it is possible.'

2

Very late that evening, when everyone else had finally gone to bed, Mike and I sat on opposite sides of the round table by the big window at the back of the sitting-room and drank a glass of wine together. Quietly but clearly through our music system, Jacqueline du Pré and Edward Elgar yet again celebrated the rich autumnal mulch of beauty and sadness offered by a world in which life, however vibrant, is inescapably a prelude to physical decline and death. I found myself tingling with something that was greater than expectation, because my tingle was born in what was happening *now*. Such immaculately mellow times were rare enough in our hectic lives, but this seemed distinctively special to me, one of those mysterious, unplanned occasions, so artlessly shaped by circumstance, and so infused with significance that each one has almost the nature of a sacrament. As I sat and sipped my wine, I thought about all that I had and all those I loved, and from there I moved to thinking about all that the swiftly passing years might do to take those things and those people away from me, or to take me away from them. Suddenly, abruptly, typically, there was no mellowness and the moment had gone. I felt like a child lost in the dark, and I was filled with dread.

'Mike,' I said in a small voice, 'is it going to be all right?'

Mike transferred his gaze to me from the one or two stars visible in the night sky through the open curtains, and raised his eyebrows.

'Is what going to be all right?'

'Everything. Is everything going to be all right?'

'Ah, I see, everything – yes, I see what you mean. Sorry, I wasn't quite sure what you meant exactly.'

'Do you think it is?'

He paused before speaking again.

'Is it definitely my turn to be sure?'

We both laughed a little at that, and Mike topped up our glasses from the dark bottle that gleamed in the light from the lamp at the centre of the table. Then he reached across to the little book-case beside the window and took down the Bible that I had put there for when visitors wanted to look something up and I wanted to look as if we always had one handy. After flicking through the pages for a second or two, he found what he wanted and began to read softly:

'"Then Jesus went with his disciples to a place called Gethsemane, and he said to them, 'Sit here while I go over there and pray.' He took Peter and the two sons of Zebedee along with him, and he began to be sorrowful and troubled. Then he said to them, 'My soul is overwhelmed with sorrow to the point of death. Stay here and keep watch with me.' Going a little farther, he fell with his face to the ground and prayed, 'Father, is everything going to be all right –?'"'

Some sweet, sorrowful element of that deliberate mis-quote seemed to wrap around us like arms, as pain and joy struggled to their inevitable climax in Elgar's great hymn of triumph and despair. Joining hands across the table, we said a short prayer for Dip, for David, for Pete and Dawn and the girls, for the rest of our family, and for each other, and then we went to bed.

Also by Adrian Plass
available from HarperCollins*Publishers:*

Stress Family Robinson

The Robinson family – mother, father, two teenage sons and a six-year-old daughter who is everyone's favourite – are a typical Christian family – or *are* they?

Does life behind the front door of the tall, thin Victorian semi-detached where they live match up to (or even resemble) the image they convey at their parish church?

The one person who knows the Robinsons almost better than they know themselves is dear Dip Reynolds – trusted friend-extraordinaire who has a few surprising secrets of her own to reveal …

The Sacred Diary of Adrian Plass
Christian Speaker Aged 45¾
Illustrated by Dan Donovan

Certainly a little older, perhaps just a tiny bit wiser, Adrian Plass was amazed when his account of 'serious spiritual experiences' in *The Sacred Diary of Adrian Plass Aged 37¾* became widely read and appreciated as a funny book! More books have followed and now he's in demand as a public speaker all over the place. As we follow him to a variety of venues the reason why Christian speakers need travelling mercies becomes abundantly clear!

Many of the characters we met in the first *Sacred Diary* are with us again – Leonard Thynn, the Flushpools, Gerald (grown up now, of course!), Adrian's wife Anne, voluptuous Gloria Marsh, Edwin (the wise church elder) and the ever-religious Richard and Doreen Cook – as well as one or two new characters; Stephanie Widgeon, for instance, who only seems to have only one thing to say …

One last question – what is a banner ripping seminar?

Father to the Man
and other stories

What is a forty-something bloke to do when he and his wife don't seem to talk any more, his teenage son is alienated from him and his best mate – reliable drinking companion for many years – suddenly and inexplicably becomes a Christian?

What do a family do when a much-loved grandparent dies unexpectedly and a freshly baked cake is discovered, obviously intended to be eaten when all were together?

These are just two of the dilemmas to be addressed among many others in this latest collection of stories from the writer who created the Sacred Diarist and *An Alien at St Wilfred's*.

A Year at St Yorick's
Collected Magazines from the
Parish of Gently Down

The Anglican parish magazine is something of a neglected art form, despite the fact that these pungently English home-spun volumes of local news and views must have been read, or at least skimmed, by millions of readers every week for years and years. Adrian Plass has sought to remedy this deficiency by collecting together a whole year's worth of 'The Skull', a magazine produced for the benefit of the good people of St Yorick's, Gently Down.

In *A Year at St Yorick's* Adrian Plass, an Anglican himself, explores the intriguing world of parish life with typically serious humour and compassion. From struggling obituaries and blinkered book reviews to subtly vindictive reports on Ladies' Circle meetings, here is a must for students and connoisseurs of that most fascinating study of all – real life.

Adrian Plass Classics
The Growing Up Pains of Adrian Plass
View from a Bouncy Castle
Cabbages for the King

Adrian Plass's unique perspective on life and faith can be enjoyed once more in this omnibus edition of three of his best-selling books. In *The Growing Up Pains of Adrian Plass*, we meet the real Adrian Plass, as opposed to his fictional counterpart in the Sacred Diary series. *Cabbages for the King* and *View from a Bouncy Castle* are collections of stories, sketches and poems which celebrate both the profundity and the absurdity of life, while making keen points about the gospel. Underlying Adrian's irrepressible humour is his passionate conviction that God embraces us in our weakness and vulnerability, and that we need to gain a child-like perspective in order to understand just how much he loves us.

Christian Books

Timeless truths in shifting times

www.christian-publishing.com

News from a Christian perspective

Exclusive author interviews

Read extracts from the latest books

Share thoughts and faith

Complete list of signing events

Full catalogue & ordering

www.christian-publishing.com